Southern Wid

Brandy L Cunningh

This book is dedicated to M, and to everyone who has ever been in a situation where their right to say no to sexual conduct has been violated. This is for those of you trying to heal. Don't give up on real love.

I would like to give a huge thank you to Catherine Rupke and Literally Perfect Editing for all of your help! Your suggestions were spot-on and you have a keen eye for details!

Also by Brandy L Cunningham:

Dragonfly's Mist (Book One)

Dragonfly's Mist (Book Two) Awakening

Laying Down Roots

CONTENTS

-1-

"What can I say about Emmy? That is a difficult question to answer. I suppose I must start from the beginning. You had better make yourself comfortable, Mr. Galway."

Westley studied the woman from where he sat. Vadetta Everhart was the epitome of an older southern woman of important social standing-not a strand out of place in her perfectly coiffed silver hair, dark dress pants complemented her light pink silk blouse, and her face, made up expertly with only a touch of makeup.

Vadetta's eyes strayed to the distant yard as she seemed to compose herself and prepare for the answer. Above them, the long wispy branches of an old willow swayed in the southern breeze.

Beyond, the vast lawns of the old plantation house shimmered deep green. The house itself was a sprawling white affair that seemed erected from another era entirely. It was clear the house was well taken care of, but had been kept in its original design to preserve the historical appeal.

Vadetta Everhart studied the young man seated on the lounge chair before her. The man was certainly handsome, in a rugged masculine way. His vivid green eyes held a touch of sadness in them, but otherwise, the man was polite and friendly. His suit pulled tight across his shoulders, hinting at the well-developed muscle beneath the silk shirt. Vadetta thought he looked more like the hands-on type than a writer.

As Vadetta took a deep breath, Westley turned his attention back to the woman.

"Emmy was always ......difficult. Even as a child she seemed wild, spirited, unwilling to see the results of her actions. Her father and I did all we could to make her happy, to try to teach her the proper way, but we failed. Emmy doesn't conform to her father or me.

Even at a young age, she was distant from us. She was much closer to her brothers then she was to us. There was little understanding between us. She often spent her youth curled in front of a window, with a book, staring off into the distance. She was always daydreaming or thinking thoughts the day away.

As she got older, she only distanced herself from us more. Always off doing something or another, bringing home stray animals or orphaned wildlife. It seemed the older she became, the further her heart wandered from us. She was eight years old when she rode her first horse. The family who bought the farm neighboring ours raised Thoroughbred's. Oh, I'll never forget the day Emmy saw her first horse up close...."

Vadetta's eyes held a faraway look as though she were looking back in time at the memory itself.

"That young girl came riding down the lane on a big brown horse, and Emmy's mouth dropped open. She'd never seen a real horse up-close. She walked over there, heart on her sleeve and asked the girl if she could pat her horse. From the moment her hand touched that horse, she was in love…Oh her face. You would have thought the heavens had smiled on her."

Vadetta laughed then. Shaking her head, she continued.

"Afterward, she spent almost all of her time at the neighbors, from the moment the sun came up to well past dark. So many times her father would get upset and send her brothers to fetch her. He didn't feel it was proper for a young lady to spend all her time at a barn. I allowed it…I had seen the expression on her face that day. I knew she had found her passion.

As the years passed, our connection started to go downhill. Emmy grew wilder all the time, galloping around with that friend Pamela, of hers.. It seemed the harder her father and I tried to turn her into a proper young woman, the farther she ran. The summer she turned sixteen it all came crashing down around us. She made a bad choice about a boy and when her father and I found out, we were furious.

Emmy was always wise for her years, she had an ancientness to her that made her seem older than she was. She was the only girl in our family, so we allowed her more freedom, that summer, however, her wildness grew out of hand. The day she left, she told me she had an offer at a sponsorship, and I told her she was a fool to think he would keep his word after what she had done. I told her she was too young to go off on her own to ride horses. We said words we could not take back.

Accusations are not something easily forgotten. She left that night while we slept. I've not seen or spoken to my daughter since that day, Mr. Galway."

Westley's dark brows came together sharply. "So her decision was to leave? She just left to go riding horses?"

Smiling, Vadetta nodded. "I think it's what she had been waiting for all that time. Since seeing her first horse.

Even after she broke her arm at fourteen, after falling from a horse for the first time. She was so upset!

Having to spend nearly eight weeks cooped up. I thought maybe she would be more cautious after that, possibly even decide to stop riding horses. In truth though, it only strengthened her resolve to improve. I think I always knew she would be something great one day."

Cocking his head to one side, Westley asked, "Just what was it Mrs. Everhart, that caused her horse to throw her?"

Vadetta smiled. "She was riding with her friend through the fields jumping logs, and Emmy tried to jump an incredibly high log when her horse refused and she went flying over the side."

"Mrs. Everhart, I know you do not speak to your daughter anymore, but I was curious if you know her plans? Is she planning to take the season off? She has already missed the first two competitions and that is unusual for her. I have heard rumors that she was looking to buy a training facility."

Looking off into the distance, Vadetta shook her head. "I haven't spoken to her in all this time, Mr. Galway. Besides, I'm not exactly the person who could answer those questions. Even Pam, who I occasionally speak with would never reveal any of that to me."

Nodding, Westley studied the older woman from where he sat. He shrugged his broad shoulders.

"Yeah, I figured it was a shot in the dark. I would like to learn the answers to those questions, as I'm sure many others would as well."

"Well, Mr. Galway, why don't you ask her yourself? Pay her a visit or something?"

Westley smirked dejectedly. "I've tried that, she won't see me, says she hates meddlesome journalists. She told me to ask you anything I wanted to know about her."

Vadetta sighed. "Yes, she probably wants to test me, see what I would say. Well, other than her past I don't know much about her anymore."

"Well, Mrs. Everhart, I'd like to thank you for all your help. Everyone from the ***Southern Horse Magazine*** will be grateful."

∞∞∞∞

-2-

Emmy frowned as she read the major article in the *__Southern Horse magazine__*. The headline was tasteful, she had to admit. Reading it aloud, she shook her head. "Emmy Everhart, Jumping invisible hurdles…"

Who was this man? His article was surprisingly truthful. He hadn't made up any facts as she would have expected him to do. Reading aloud the bold words in the center of the article, Emmy realized how true the words were.

"She's been jumping invisible hurdles her whole life, never content to stay in place, and never tied down by the restraints of commitment. She only commits herself, heart and soul to her equestrian pursuit."

It was true, commitments were not her strongest virtue. The question this Mr. Galway seemed intent on answering was the direction her career was taking. Did she have a new prospect? Were the rumors of her opening a training facility true? It was what everyone was asking. Since she had taken the championship title in both cross-country and show jumping this past year, she had caught the eye of many. Emmy, however, preferred to remain out of the public eye. She didn't like prying journalists snooping about and digging into her life.

At the sound of approaching tires crunching on the gravel drive, Emmy walked out of the barn and into the bright sunlight of the day. Squinting, she watched the dark blue Chevy come down the long tree-lined drive. Behind the truck entering the drive, the large white Ford belonging to the contractor followed. Walking toward the approaching trucks, Emmy waved.

Coming out of the blue Chevy, the olive-skinned woman waved cheerfully at Emmy.

"Hey, you!! Don't look so glum, kid! Aren't you excited? This is the start of our dream. We will finally be building that big equestrian facility you and I have dreamed about all these years!"

Emmy pulled the woman into her arms for a big hug. "Ah, I know Pammy, I just don't like being around a bunch of people I don't know."

Smiling at her friend, she noticed the flush to Pam's olive skin and the light in her deep brown eyes. She wore her dark hair casually pulled up in a ponytail, complete with jeans and a tank.

"Damn Pamela, I have to say, marriage agrees with you. The two of you have only been celebrating marriage a few weeks and already you glow like a damn fairy!"

Pamela Ryans laughed her alluring laugh. "Oh, Emmy. It does. I cannot tell you how happy I am or how grateful I am to have found my David. I only wish you could be so lucky!"

Ignoring Pam's comment about her own love life, or lack of, Emmy turned to greet the two men alighting from the truck behind her friend. David came forward to pull her into a gentle hug.

"Emmy, you're looking lovely as always. So, this is the place, huh? It's great. These pastures are huge, and I see the potential it has to be a great training center for us."

David looked around, studying the small six-stall barn behind them. Turning in the opposite direction, he took in the vast lush green pastures, and finally the old Victorian farmhouse in the distance. The house was huge and sprawling with its three stories, and beautiful wrap around porch. He could easily see why Emmy had fallen in love with the place. He and Pam had been on their honeymoon when Emmy had called Pam, over the moon with excitement. She had found the perfect place for their training center.

Pam had insisted that they become partners with Emmy, saying she could never afford to keep the place up or create the facility of her dreams without their help. David had noticed the close bond between the two women from the beginning. He had known it was a dream of theirs to own a huge horse ranch since the time they had been young children. Although David did not know Emmy's history well, he had learned enough from Pam to know her past had been harsh and sad. Wanting nothing more than to please his bride, David had agreed on the partnership.

Emmy had full ownership of the house, the small barn, and the ten acres surrounding it. The Ryans and Emmy each owned equal shares in the two hundred acres of lush pastures and gentle hills that surrounded the house.

Turning back toward Emmy and Pam, David watched as Emmy greeted their passenger, Michael Fitzgerald.

"So Emmy, you ready to break ground on this facility you've waited all this time for?"

Pulling herself out of Michael's arms, Emmy smiled at him.

Turning toward David, she said, "Hell yes, I'm ready David."

Seated on the porch, Emmy watched the Contractor and David as they made their plans for the new barn, and arena's they would soon be building.

"The company I've hired to put in all the welded pipe fencing around the property, as well as build the turn out shelters should be arriving tomorrow morning."

Pam nodded. "Goodness Emmy, can you believe it's all finally happening? I can still remember being ten years old and lying out in the fields on my daddy's farm... just dreaming of all this!"

Laughing, Emmy smiled reminiscently. "Yeah, I know. I don't know if I ever thought this would all come true. Especially after..."

"Oh no you don't, Emmy we are not going down that road right now, okay. I never doubted we would get here. We just had a few speed bumps along the way. "

Nodding her agreement, Emmy rotated to look at Pam and Michael.

"Yeah. Speed bumps. Pam, Michael, I owe the two of you so damn much. Pam, you've always been there for me, you believed in me, even when I didn't know the front of a horse from the rear. And Michael, if you hadn't convinced Mr. Montgomery to come watch me ride I would never have gotten the sponsorship that landed me here."

Michael laughed. "Oh Emmy, I will never forget the day you plodded your sorry worn-out hide into my barn, telling me you needed a job. Whether it was shoveling horse manure or riding, it didn't matter and you were not taking no for an answer."

Laughing with the others, Emmy sighed fondly. She loved these two with all that was left of her heart. About to say so, she turned toward them but stopped when she noticed a silver pickup coming down the drive.

"Either of you expecting company?"

Pam looked up and remembered her phone call earlier that afternoon.

"Oh, uh," Clearing her throat nervously, Pam smiled guiltily at Emmy.

"Oh boy, you're going to hate me, but I accepted an interview on your behalf."

17

Emmy stared at her friend in horror. "My god, Pam please tell me you didn't! Even worse you allowed them to come here? To my home! Oh my god, I am so going to kill you for this!"

"No, just wait Em. Look, this guy, he wrote that article I told you about. It was good. He wrote it with taste and with the truth. This could be good for us, and good for this place. Just give him a chance. If you don't like the questions he asks or anything else we will send him on his way, okay?"

Glaring at her friend, Emmy huffed. "Fine. But you are still dead."

Emmy turned her attention to the man who had just hopped from the truck and was heading toward them. Although she couldn't see much except his silhouette, Emmy was caught off guard by what she did see. Having expected a willowy older man as was the typical journalist, Emmy couldn't help but notice this man's tall broad physique. The closer he came, the more Emmy found herself surprised.

Stopping just in front of the porch, the man looked straight at Emmy.

"Hello, I am Westley Galway. Ms. Everhart, I cannot express how grateful I am that you have agreed to this interview."

Arching a delicate auburn eyebrow, Emmy studied the man before her. There was only one way to describe him. Darkly handsome. This man was not what Emmy would have pictured. He stood around six-foot, with a broad muscular build, but not the build you get from going to the gym. No, this man looked like a man used to hard work. His dark hair was slightly wavy and a little shaggy, but this only added to his charm. His face was strong and masculine, with a slight five o' clock shadow, and the most striking pair of deep-green eyes Emmy had ever seen.

Westley Galway looked more like someone that belonged on the cover of G.Q. magazine than someone writing for one.

"Well, Mr. Galway, I'm afraid I did not agree to this interview, but since you're here, I will cooperate as long as I get to approve everything before it's published."

Westley found himself surprised by the bite in Emmy's voice.

"Ah... Well, I'm sorry about whoever tricked you into this meeting, I arranged it with..."

Before Westley could continue, the olive-skinned woman beside Emmy held up her hand.

"Mr. Galway, I am Pamela Ryans, or, well you probably know me as Pamela Walker, I am the one you spoke with earlier, and I agreed to the interview. My partner Emmy has graciously agreed to see you, even though I did trick her into this, so I apologize if she turns into an ogre on you. Please try not to take it personally."

Westley was a little surprised. "Ah...yes, Pamela Walker. I know who you are. I must say however, I was unaware that you and Ms. Everhart were...uh that is... that you were partners. I uh..."

Pamela tried and failed to contain her laughter. It bubbled out of her. "Oh dear, Mr. Galway, I'm afraid that didn't come out right...We are business partners, not partner...partners...you know?"

Westley sighed in relief and felt like a total fool. "Ah, well I must say I'm glad we cleared that up. Forgive me for assuming. There would have been nothing wrong with that, I just..." Westley felt like a jerk at this point.

Pam smiled and studied Westley. It had not escaped her notice the way his eyes kept seeking out Emmy. His gaze roved over her with appreciation. Clearly, he found her friend attractive.

Smiling mischievously, Pam said, "Come, Mr. Galway take a seat and let's get this interview started."

Westley took a chair across from the other three and laid out his notebook, tape recorder, and other supplies on the table.

"So, Ms. Everhart, I have a couple questions I would like to start with if that's okay?"

At Emmy's nod, he continued. "Well, first, since I'm sitting here I'm going to guess the rumors are true about you starting a training facility?"

Emmy nodded. "Yes, Pam Ryans and I are planning to build a full equestrian training center within the next couple years. As you know this is a long procedure so I can't give you an exact date."

"Well, that's exciting. Will this training center be strictly for your personal horses, or will you be opening it to boarding and clients as well?"

Emmy shrugged. "No decisions are final yet. We've talked about bringing in horses owned by others to train and show, about the possibility of giving lessons, breeding and sales, but again we have yet to decide."

Westley studied the young woman before him, trying to compare her to her mother whom he had recently interviewed. He quickly realized there were few likenesses. Vadetta Everhart displayed poise, considering everything with great care, Emmy Everhart seemed passionate, answering as she saw fit, rather than taking time to consider her alternatives. She held herself with pride, and it was easy to see the wild willful young woman her mother had described.

"You have not been at the competitions this season. There are many speculations about your plans. Is Viewfinder still going to be competing?"

Emmy smiled. "Viewfinder is in perfect health, he is in the prime of his career and we look forward to returning to the competitions. Right now, however, I need to focus on getting this place up and running, so I have decided to give Viewfinder a light year, and allow him to be a stud for the first time. I am excited to see what his progeny holds."

Westley mumbled to himself as he sorted through the notes he had taken in his interview earlier that afternoon. Emmy Everhart had not been what he had expected at all. He found himself enchanted by the auburn-haired beauty as well as the Victorian house she called home. He had seen her from afar in the past and had heard mention of her good looks, but he had not expected what he found. She was beyond pretty. Beautiful did not even begin to describe her. She was…wild. Untamed. Exquisite.

Westley sighed at himself. He was no boy. He had been around good-looking women before, but there was something about Emmy Everhart that had him feeling expectant, excited and emotional all at the same time. This wasn't the first time he'd had this reaction to the woman. The first time he had seen her ride, about eight months prior, he had been on his first assignment as a journalist.

Covering the Blue Meadows Grand Prix had been his assignment. It was there that he had watched Emmy fly over the jumps on that chestnut stallion. Horse and rider were a magnetic duo. The way they moved together it seemed as though the two had one mind. He had seen good riders in his time. Came from an entire family of equestrians, but seeing her in motion had touched something deep within him. Something he had thought buried with his brother.

It felt too close to home. The way she had made him feel with every stride, every leap, and landing, he could have counted the strides as though it were him up on that chestnut stallion. Just like he had felt when he had watched Joseph. Shaking his head, Westley slammed his fist down on the table in front of him.

"Dammit Joseph! Why couldn't you just listen to me? I told you that bloody horse was no' ready!"

Striding across the room, Westley fought the urge to drink. He had tried to drink the memory of that day away with alcohol, but that had made him angry. Then, he had left his home, the one place he had always loved. He had thought America was the right decision, so how did he end right back in the middle of that damn sport? How did he end up looking into the broken blue eyes of a woman that stirred his blood in a way no other female ever had?

Staring off into the rainstorm outside, Westley wondered what it had been that he had seen in her dark blue eyes. There had been something there, something broken-the woman's past held demons-and Westley could imagine it had something to do with the event that severed her ties with her family. In all the time he had been working for the magazine he had yet to see her with a man.

Clearly, her past was full of emotional pain. He remembered the look in her eyes, that to most people would be invisible, but for some reason, Westley had seen past the fortress and into the pain. He imagined she wore her cold persona to keep others away. She had baggage. He had baggage. Clearly, this connection or whatever it was he had felt for her would never work out.

Westley could imagine all too well holding that spitfire in his arms, feeling her curves pressing into him… He had to stop this. From that moment on, Westley swore he would stay away from Emmy Everhart. He would finish this assignment, and then it was time to move on. He'd find another state, another job if he must. The distance was what he needed.

∞∞∞∞∞

-3-

Pam watched Emmy as she went about her chores. David had finally finished with the contractor and headed to her side.

"Hey baby, why the pensive look?"

Shrugging, Pam studied her husband. David had chased her for nearly two years before she had finally given in and gone on a date with him. She had never been more grateful for anything than the decision to allow this man into her heart.

"The journalist who came out today wasn't what I had expected. I don't think he was what Emmy expected either. I feel confident when I say I felt an attraction between the two straight away. But you know Emmy, she shut it down just as soon as she realized. God, I hate what she went through because of her family and that disgusting pig.

I honestly don't know if she will ever let a man into her life in that way, David. And that scares me. It makes me so sad to think that someone as wonderful as Emmy may never know what it's like to have someone love her the way you love me."

David pulled his wife into his arms. Wiping the moisture from her eyes, he leaned down to kiss her neck.

"I may not know the full story of what happened to her when you guys were younger, but I'm not blind. I see the way she shudders whenever any man she doesn't know comes near her. I see the way her eyes go cold when men try to flirt with her. That pain takes more than just time to heal. It takes the right person.

Every person has their own path, their own destiny in life. Some people never marry, and never have a family, but happiness is possible. I've seen the way she is with those horses, and I think that her path may lie with them. Maybe she will find the right man to help her along, but it will take time. Pammy baby. But we will always be here to help her along her way."

Pam leaned into her husband's arms and kissed him deeply.

Looking up into David's hazel eyes, she whispered, "You have no idea how amazing you are. I am blessed to have you."

Emmy leaned back against the stall where her beloved Viewfinder munched his grain contentedly. Studying the couple on her porch across the way, Emmy sighed heavily. She was happy that Pam had found such a wonderful man, but deep in her heart, an emptiness ached where all the pieces were missing. Once, long ago she had wished for the perfect marriage and a perfect family. She'd had such big fairy tale dreams of how her life would be. She would marry her brother's best friend, and they would live happily ever after.

That happily ever after turned into a dark nightmare for her when that boy had shown his evilness. He had ruined Emmy in the most disgusting way possible. He had taken her childhood crush and smashed it with his fist over and over. Emmy knew if she had gone to someone that night, with the bruises still obvious all over her chest and torso they would have believed her. Instead, she had hidden away in fear. Then, when she had finally worked up the nerve to tell someone, it was too late, no one believed her. They all turned their backs on her.

Emmy swore that was the last time anyone would hurt her like that. No man would ever touch her again, and she would never be weak and afraid again. Love was not her priority. She would spend her days alone. Behind her, the stallion snorted in contempt and rattled his bucket. Turning toward the deep chestnut stallion, Emmy smiled.

"What's wrong, buddy? You inhale all your grain too fast, and now you have none left?"

The stallion shook his head and pushed his muzzle into her neck. Wiggling his top lip the stallion whinnied.

Laughing, Emmy scratched his neck. "You big flirt. You think just because you sweet talk me I'll give you more?"

Reaching into her pocket, Emmy produced two sugar cubes. Viewfinder munched noisily on them, nodding his head in happiness.

Over the next few months, workers came and went from the property, starting construction on the new barn and arenas. Fencing ran around the whole ranch, dividing the acreage into pastures. Each pasture had an alley which separated pastures and paddocks, making it easier to keep stallions contained, as well as feeding and moving horses to and from. Shelters stood in all the outer paddocks and pastures. Emmy had be-gun slowly working on the house, restoring and repairing, as well as moving in furniture to make the huge eight bedroom house feel more like a home.

This was the first place she had thought of as home since leaving her parents at sixteen. Above the fireplace mantel sat the portrait of the tiny baby girl. Every morning Emmy would stop to kiss the picture of the daughter she hadn't been allowed to keep. Swallowing the tears that would threaten to overwhelm her, she would go about her day and try to form some likeness of a life. Being here alone with all these strange men coming and going did little to ease Emmy's apprehension over starting the ranch.

She longed to be back in the show ring where she could feel the wind around her and the power of her horse beneath her. Every morning, Emmy took View-finder on a ride through their sprawling hills. It was the only way for her to stay sane. It was on one such morning ride that Emmy found a big disheveled dog sleeping in the barn. At first, she was weary, the dog had to be well over one-hundred pounds. Just visible through the clumps of mud, the dog's brown fur held many stickers and brambles.

Emmy thought about calling Animal Control, but then the dog turned its dirty face toward her and peered at her with the most soulful soft brown eyes. Emmy felt her heart soften toward the poor beast. Taking a tentative step toward the dog, she held out her hand and called to the dog. Crouching down in what she hoped would be a non-threatening stance, she tried again. Slowly, the dog shifted toward her. Its sad eyes watched her, not trusting her. Emmy sighed.

"Come on baby, it's okay sweetheart, I promise I won't hurt you. You just have to trust me."

Ever so slowly the dog came forward. Always keeping its body lowered, close to the ground and trying to avoid eye contact, it crept submissively toward Emmy in a way that broke her heart. It was clear the dog's treatment had been poor, and Emmy felt the moisture sting her eyes as she watched the massive dog crawl toward her.

When finally the dog reached her, Emmy slowly extended her hand, nearly sobbing when the poor animal winced as her hand brushed gently across its shoulder. Emmy gritted her teeth in anger that someone could reduce this giant dog into a simpering pile of fear.

Slowly stroking and speaking in soothing tones, Emmy lowered herself onto the floor and continued to stroke the dog's dirty fur soothingly. After about twenty minutes, the dog slowly crawled into Emmy's lap and let go a giant sigh of relief. Tears now stained both of Emmy's cheeks at the torture of the poor soul.

"Emmy, you here? Hey, this place is looking good. You've been busy. I bought you one of those Fu Fu coffee drinks you like…a latte? Anyway…I read the article from the interview. He did a bang-up job. I mean I like that guy's style… OH MY GOD!"

Coming around the corner into the downstairs bathroom where she had heard voices, Pam came to an abrupt halt at the sight that greeted her. Emmy was on her knees in front of the tub, hosing down a giant muddy animal resembling a bear, or a wolf, she wasn't sure at this point. Staring from Emmy to the animal, Pam wasn't sure which one was in worst shape at this point.

"What the hell is that thing, and why on earth do you have it in the bathtub?"

Turning to grin at Pam, Emmy said, "Pam, meet Rainy. Rainy, meet Pam. She's your other momma. Pam, I found her out in the barn this morning in the rainstorm, the poor creature was cowering in a corner and I just couldn't call someone to come take her away."

Pam grimaced. "That thing's a she? Looks more like Bigfoot. Maybe it's got an owner out there looking for it."

Shaking her head, Emmy's jaw clenched. "Well if they ever show up here looking for her all they're likely to meet is the barrel of my Remington. You should have seen how the poor baby flinched when I touched her. It made me so sad. I can't send her away Pammy. She's covered in stickers and mud, and I think this black stuff might be tar…"

Pam sighed. She thought the dog was a charity case they could not help. There was, however, a light in Emmy's eyes Pam hadn't seen in a long time. Sighing again, Pam shrugged. If it made her friend happy then what the hell. Walking up to the animal, she slowly extended her hand. She noticed immediately the way the dog slunk away from her in fear. Feeling her own protectiveness flare, Pam lowered herself to the mat beside Emmy and spoke in soothing tones until the dog was leaning into the lathering and scrubbing from both women.

David found them an hour later, towels were strewn about the bathroom, both women soaked through, and beneath the towels, the biggest German shepherd he'd ever seen. As he stepped into the bathroom, three pairs of eyes turned toward him. The dog's lips pulled back in a snarl as it tried to place itself between the two women it had claimed as its pack, and the man she felt was a threat.

Emmy jumped to her feet. "Rainy, no! You will not harm David. He is a friend. It's okay girl."

As she spoke, Emmy slowly put herself between David and the dog she called Rainy. Slowly, the dog relaxed and let the snarl slip from her lips. She kept her gaze on David but made no other attempt at aggression. Emmy rubbed the dog's red and black head lovingly.

"That's a good girl. Protectiveness is ok, it's good, but David is a friend. There's a good girl."

Turning toward David, Emmy continued. "Sorry David, she hasn't had the best treatment, and she'll come around. She just needs time."

David smiled. "I'm going to go get some meat from the kitchen. Judging by her ribs I think that will go a long way in helping her trust me."

Emmy looked over the new shoots of lush green grass coming up in her front yard. Weeds and unkempt garden beds abounded here, just waiting for her attention. It was one feature she had liked about the property. The chance to take the place and make it her own. While the construction was underway on the barn and arenas, she busied herself making the home she had always dreamed of.

Walking around the back with the shaggy Rainy following close at her heels, she surveyed the once grand garden that now stood in dying disrepair. The dried dead stalks of rosebushes were scattered throughout the perimeter and the stone fountain in the center had seen better days. Finding the wrought iron bench amid all the ruin, she sat down. Allowing herself to study the house and garden around her, Emmy sucked in a deep cleansing breath.

Finally, after so many years she had a place she could belong. No more staying in barn apartments belonging to whichever trainer she was currently riding for. Now, she was the trainer, and she would ride under her own name. She had a house all to herself, and a farm that was more than she ever dreamed possible. It would be a few years yet before it was a functioning training stable, but in her mind, she could already see it.

She could imagine the colts romping in the pastures beside their dams, and the students riding in the arenas. She could see her future here without any fear or anxiety. Perhaps now she could finally move on and put the past behind her. Many years now she had carried the pain and guilt of that day on her shoulders. As much as she told herself it was not her fault, she still felt the blame lay with herself.

Perhaps if she had not been so headstrong, perhaps if she had not allowed herself to trust in a friend, she wouldn't have gone through that. There was no use now trying to see through the what if's of life. She could never undo what happened. She had tried over the years to forget, to move on, even to allow herself to think about the possibility of dating, but it never panned out.

Every time she spoke to a man, she felt nothing. No attraction, none of the desire other women often described. She felt cold, dead. As though she no longer had the ability to feel for a man. Maybe that part of herself was not something she could repair. She had started to believe it was, that is, until the day she had met Westley Galway. The moment she had looked up into his intense green eyes, she had experienced things she'd never felt.

Heat, need desire. The feelings had hit her with an intensity that had caught her off guard. When she had looked into those eyes, she had the overwhelming feeling of calm, safety, as though she had known this man all of her life. Even now, several weeks later, when she sat here in her decaying garden, just the image of him in her mind sent her body into a frenzy of feelings she was not familiar with.

Whatever it was about Westley, Emmy was grateful she didn't have an excuse to see him again. She wasn't sure how to react to the feelings he elicited from her. Standing, Emmy stretched her long legs. She knew exactly what to do with all the pent of feelings that man had left welled up within her. Heading toward the clump of dead rosebushes, she put on her gloves and began yanking the stalks from the ground with enthusiasm.

Westley studied the picture in front of him. It was the cover of a magazine featuring Emmy on the front page as she glided over an incredibly big water jump at her latest cross-country event. According to the article, she had recently returned to the eventing circuit after a year off. She and Viewfinder had quickly worked their way back into the top spot. Not surprising at all. The pair looked great. Seemingly, the year off had done them good.

The article talked about the huge equestrian facility she and Pamela Ryans were planning to open within the next year or two. According to the author, the facility would offer full-scale training, lessons, and breeding.

Emmy Everhart and Pamela Ryans would both be offering lessons and training. In addition, Emmy's stallion had sired four foals this year, all healthy and showing much potential. Sighing and leaning back in the chair in which he sat, Westley smiled to himself. She looked amazing flying through the air on that big chestnut stallion. Westley wanted nothing more than to see Emmy again, but he knew that would be a mistake.

She had demons in her life to face, an equestrian facility to get started, and he had a past full of sadness to sort through. Glancing down at the plane ticket lying on the table, Westley allowed himself to revisit the lush green hills of his birthplace. He missed Ireland incredibly. He had been away for six years, and now he was about to go back. As much as Westley wasn't ready to face the demons in his past, his mother was ill and nothing would keep him away from her.

Glancing down at the picture of Emmy on the magazine cover one last time, he swore he would see her again. Tucking the magazine into his pack, Westley paid his tab and headed toward the airport. Toward Ireland. Away from Emmy Everhart and those intoxicating blue eyes of hers.

Walking through the crowd toward the escalators, Westley tried to push his way through without being too rude. He hated crowded cities where people shoved without thought, where people lost the side of humanity that called for caring and compassion. He knew to respect others, but here in America, it seemed easier and easier to just become one of the crowd and push his way through.

Glancing down at his watch, Westley took his eyes off the crowd for a second. In that instant, he was shoved forward, colliding with the woman walking toward him. Cursing under his breath, Westley hauled himself up and reached for the woman who'd landed in front of him.

"I am truly sorry ma'am, people at the airport are worse than cattle I'm telling you. Are you hurt?"

The woman laughed and took Westley's arm. As he turned to pull her up, Westley found himself staring into a vivid blue gaze.

"I'm quite all right, thank you."

When Westley realized just who it was lying in front of him, he couldn't have been more surprised if he had been struck by lightning. Of all the people in the immense world, there sat Emmy Everhart. As Emmy looked up into the man's startlingly familiar green eyes, recognition suddenly hit her and she laughed.

"Ah, Mr. Galway, what a surprise…that is unless you've been following me, I've heard journalists can be incredibly sneaky."

Westley laughed. "Well I've heard that as well, but actually, I'm not a journalist anymore. Haven't been for a while now. So, if I'm stalking you it's for an entirely selfish reason." Westley grinned at her, hoping she wouldn't take his comment for more than the joke it was.

Emmy studied Westley Galway, and she was immediately struck again by how handsome this man was. She was acutely aware of her intense attraction to this man, and it made her extremely uneasy. He had only ever been polite and even charming toward her, so she knew it was ridiculous to feel so unnerved around him. Laughing slightly, Emmy quirked a brow at him.

"So, Mr. Galway, You gonna help a woman up off the ground, or stand there staring at me?"

Westley immediately felt like a complete idiot. Pulling Emmy up toward him, he was so nervous about seeing her again he put a little too much power into the pull, unintentionally yanking her right up against his chest. Groaning quietly, he gently moved her away from him.

Running his hand through his hair he sighed, "Geez, I'm sorry Emmy, I didn't realize how light you were."

Emmy studied the man in front of her. The oddest thing had happened to her when she had crashed into his chest. Instead of the typical fear she usually felt when around men she didn't know, Emmy felt over-whelming feelings of sensuality. As though all her nerve endings were on fire everywhere that Westley's skin had touched hers. Watching him, Emmy couldn't help but notice the way he seemed almost nervous around her. Westley did not seem like a man who experienced nerves around women. And to top that off, the way he had said her name was almost like a caress.

Shaking her head, Emmy told herself now was not the time to lose her mind.

Stepping around Westley so she was again facing him she said, "So, assuming you were joking earlier about the whole stalker thing…. What are you doing at the airport?"

Westley tried to compose himself, but looking into those blue depths was like losing his mind.

"I'm heading back to Ireland. My mother is ill."

Emmy's face softened slightly. "Oh, I'm so sorry to hear that Westley. I wish her well. I thought you had an accent last time we spoke."

"Yes, born and raised in Ireland. Although it has faded a bit in the six years I've been here in the states. How about you? What brings you to the airport?"

Emmy smiled. "Well, I am actually on my way to see a horse…incidentally enough, I'm headed to Ireland as well."

Westley shook his head, now he knew he must be dreaming. "Ireland huh? Why all the way to Ireland? Last I saw Viewfinder was in the top of his career, surely you don't need a replacement."

"No, no, Viewfinder is great. Not a replacement, actually. It is a couple of broodmare's and a colt I've had an offer to buy and I've always held a fascination with the Irish Draught. I guess you're used to them though, having grown up in Ireland after all."

Nodding his head, Westley said, "Ah, yes the Draughts. Great horses. I'm quite familiar with the breed. So, I don't suppose we are on the same flight?"

Just then, the call for Westley's flight announced boarding. Looking over at Emmy, he said, "Well, we better hurry if we don't want to miss that flight huh?"

Seated on the plane, Westley couldn't believe Emmy sat only two rows back and to the left of him. He had sworn to avoid her for the past year, even quit his job and moved to another state just to keep himself from trying to pursue a relationship with her. That she was here, headed to Ireland at this particular time made him pause. Was this fate? Should he ask her to lunch or dinner? Should he take advantage of this crazy chance meeting with her? Westley was at a loss. On the one hand, he was unsure which action to take with Emmy. On the other, he could not ignore the worry he felt for his mother.

A few rows off, Emmy studied the back of Westley's head. Why did she feel these odd stirrings whenever he was near? She had not felt attraction to a man since she was sixteen years old. Was this something just between the two of them, or was this just a sign telling her she needed to allow herself to have another chance with men? What was it about Westley that she found so appealing anyway? Emmy chuckled to herself.

That one was easy. Everything. The man exuded sexual appeal. He was good-looking in a darkly mysterious way, and yet his personality was open and friendly. Charming actually. Groaning, Emmy decided it would be best to avoid Westley from this point on. He was a complication she couldn't and wouldn't allow into her life right now.

Hours later, Emmy made her way off the plane, trying her best to avoid Westley, but trying not to be obvious about it. She didn't know why she was suddenly feeling these emotions, but she decided now was not the time to act on them. Just outside the airport, Emmy had herself convinced she had managed to avoid Westley Galway when she heard someone clear their throat behind her. Whirling around, she sighed. There he was, grinning at her in that way of his.

"Emmy, do you need a lift somewhere? I'd be happy to drop you off along the way. It would be no trouble. I'd feel better knowing you were going to be all right in an unfamiliar country."

Emmy studied Westley. She should say no. She should decline.

Opening her mouth to refuse his offer, Emmy heard herself say, "Ok, sure." What the hell? Hadn't she just convinced herself it was better to stay away from Westley? She really needed to get her priorities straight.

Seated beside Westley, Emmy fidgeted. Westley watched her fidget and it was easy enough to see that he made her nervous. What was it about him that riled her up so much?

Glancing at her as he maneuvered the car through the country roads, Westley asked, "Why do you seem uncomfortable around me, Emmy?"

Emmy looked up at Westley in surprise. "I'm not uncomfortable with you, Westley, I uh, I just get the feeling that you're interested in something from me that I'm not interested in."

There. Even if it wasn't true, that should put some space between them and cool off any attraction he had toward her.

Westley sat in silence for several moments. That was not exactly what he had expected. She didn't seem like a conceited person to him, but the way she had just said that left him wondering.

"Exactly what is it that you think I'm interested in Emmy?"

Emmy frowned. He seemed a little irritated at her words, and that brought back memories of another man…Shaking the thought away, Emmy thought, I will not go there.

Shifting in her seat toward Westley, she said, "Look, Mr. Galway, you seem like a decent guy and all, but I'm not interested in anything, or any relationship right now."

Westley lifted a brow at her. "Who said anything about a relationship? I won't deny that I'm attracted to you Emmy, you're a beautiful woman. However, I don't exactly hear myself professing love ballets or asking for commitment."

Misinterpreting his words, Emmy stared in anger at him. "Excuse me, Mr. Galway, but if you think I'm a one-night stand kind of woman then you are quite delusional. I appreciate the ride, but once you've dropped me, I will be happy never to hear from you again." Emmy turned to stare out her window.

Westley held in a curse. This conversation had gone all wrong. How the hell had she interpreted it that he just wanted a night in the sack with her? That was the last thought on his mind.

"Look Emmy…"

Emmy held up her hand to silence him. "This conversation is over, Mr. Galway." Westley clenched his teeth in annoyance. The woman was too stubborn for her own good.

Entering the town of Killarney, where Emmy had asked him to drop her off, Westley decided he could not, would not let her leave with this misinterpretation between them. Glancing her way, he studied her stony silhouette in silence. He needed to fix things between them. He knew that it would eat at him if he left these things so unresolved.

"Emmy, I know we may have started off on the wrong road today, but I want to clarify things between us..."

"Mr. Galway, there is no need..."

"Emmy. Please. Just hear me out, alright. I cannot say that I am not attracted to you. You are a beautiful woman, but I am not looking for a relationship right now. I find you interesting, I enjoy speaking with you, but that is as far as it goes. I also have no intent to try to get you in the sack."

Emmy studied the handsome man seated beside her for a few minutes. Finally, she nodded her head.

"Ok, Mr. Galway. I will accept that you have no interest in me at all. Thank you, for clearing that one up."

Westley watched in aggravation as she once again turned her stone-cold façade toward the window. He clenched and unclenched his jaws, praying for patience.

"Emmy. Why do you take offense to everything I say? Look, why don't we have a bite to eat together, and try to start again. Maybe then you'll see I'm not the ogre you have me made out to be."

Emmy wanted to say no, she did. Her stomach, however, had other ideas. She was starving, and her stomach groaned loudly at the mention of food.

Laughing, Westley lifted a brow. "Is that a yes, you'll come and have dinner with me, strictly platonic, two people, acquaintances who happen to be traveling together?"

Eyeing the intolerable man, Emmy sighed.

"Alright. I guess it couldn't hurt. If you piss me off, however, then that will be it, and I'll walk the rest of the way."

Seated at the small table near the window of the friendly pub located on the corner of the main street, Westley again found himself studying Emmy's profile. She was beautiful. It wasn't in a traditional way either. Many times, society and people in general classified a woman beautiful based on her looks, her figure, the makeup she wore, or her sense of fashion. Yet, here sat this lovely country girl, dressed in her faded blue jeans, and a tank top, with a button up flannel over the top.

Her deep auburn hair hung in a loose braid, with a few daring strands escaping to hang loosely around her face. She had not one stitch of makeup on and seemingly could care less about what anyone thought. Her skin was smooth and clear like ivory, with a touch of golden from her days in the sun. Her lashes were long and dark coppery colored, framing her large dark blue eyes.

She had a sexy figure, the kind you get from years working with and riding horses. She was lean and strong, but with the gentle curves, Westley appreciated. He had never liked women to be too thin. He preferred women who enjoyed working outside and were not afraid of a little dirt. Emmy fit that bill too well. Sighing, he turned away, glad for the distraction when their food came. It was difficult not to feel the rising attraction to this woman as he sat here looking at her.

Emmy was not oblivious to Westley's intense studying of her. She tried to play it off like she did not notice. Like she did not feel the heat of those alluring green eyes as they traced their path over her face and body. She had to fight the gooseflesh that threatened to rise everywhere his eyes looked. Why was it this man's gaze felt like a caress? Shaking off the feeling, Emmy felt relief when their food came.

Watching as Westley bit into his food with gusto, Emmy asked, "So, Westley, you're from Ireland. What was it like growing up here?"

Westley swallowed his food, shrugging his shoulders. "The same as everywhere else I guess, just a different accent." He grinned when Emmy laughed. God that sound was enough to make him want to kiss her right then and there.

Emmy sent him an amused look. "Seriously? Did you grow up in the city or the country?"

Westley smiled indulgently at her. "The country. My family owns a farm not too far from here. I admit I'm procrastinating. You must think me a terrible person."

Emmy tilted her head as she studied the sadness she could see in Westley's eyes. "No, not necessarily. I only know your mom is sick, not whether you should be on your way post-haste."

Westley ran his fingers through his hair, something Emmy had seen him do at their first meeting. Something that stirred her blood. Clearing her throat, she took a bite of food, trying to distract her body from the heat coursing through it.

"My sister called yesterday. She said my mum's been sick, but they just got the diagnosis that she had cancer. The doctor thinks we'll be lucky if we get six months. I have never believed in their estimations when it comes to the human life. It's about whether someone wants to keep going, and whether they're ready to go. I plan to stay here in Ireland, to be with her until she goes.

Once, I loved Ireland, loved it with everything in my soul, but over the last decade, I've lost so much here, faced so much grievance. I feel like there is always death awaiting me here. It's soured me to my own country."

Emmy felt a chill at his soulful words. She could easily see the sadness in his eyes, and she imagined his heartbreak to feel so forlorn in a country he had once loved so dearly. She had the urge to reach out and touch him, to offer what comfort she could. She didn't, however. She didn't understand the feelings welling up for this man, but she felt to touch him would be a mistake.

Instead, she smiled understandingly at him. "I'm sorry, Westley. It is never easy to feel so much pain about something that meant so much to you in the past."

Glancing up into the deep blue of her eyes, Westley nodded. "I sense that you know a lot about pain, Emmy. The way you keep yourself cold, you avoid deep friendships, and what I've heard from your mother about your childhood. That must be hard, being so alone all the time."

Just like that, Westley watched the friendliness fade from Emmy's eyes. He knew instantly he had made a mistake bringing up her past. Immediately, he experienced regret to see her expression harden.

"You know nothing about my life, or my past, Mr. Galway. You think that just because you listened to the words my mother fed you that you know a damn thing about me? Well, you're wrong. You know nothing about me, and you never will."

Westley sighed. "Emmy, please I didn't mean to upset you. Please, calm down, forget what I said."

Standing, Emmy laid some money on the table. "Thank you for dinner, Mr. Galway. It was almost enjoyable. Almost. Good luck with your mom."

Westley watched in shock as Emmy strode out of the pub, chin held up as though she had just faced off with an enemy. He sighed again. How he always managed to mess things up with the one woman who stirred his blood like no other, he would never understand. Staring out the window until she was long gone, Westley wanted to kick himself. He should have gone after her. Why was he such a fool, to just sit here as she walked out of his life? Westley hoped he had not just ruined the only chance he'd ever have with Emmy.

∞∞∞∞

-4-

Three years later....

Emmy studied the solid black colt bounding around the field next to his dam. His long strides swallowed the ground as he frolicked and played with the liver chestnut filly. The colt, Viewfinder's Fire was elegant and high-spirited. His sister, Viewfinder's Perfection was graceful and quiet. Both foals were out of prosperous mares Emmy had invested in. Both previously shown with faultless bloodlines full of champions. Two years prior, the two mares had produced two exceptional colts which she had sold as yearlings to help makeup costs for buying the two mares.

The two foals striding across the field in front of her were equally exceptional as the previous two, but Emmy had even higher expectations for this pair. She was already attached to the two foals and knew selling them would be difficult. The past winter,

Emmy had decided it may be time to consider retiring Viewfinder to stud. The sixteen-year-old was still in excellent condition, but ten years of hard jumping could take their toll on a horse's joints. Emmy felt she owed it to the stallion to allow him his rest before it was too late. She had decided she'd rather stop now while he was still healthy.

"Mighty fine foals you've got there, girl. I have to admit this pair is even better than the last. You going to keep these two?" Pam smiled fondly as she watched the black colt nibble on the chestnut filly's ears.

"Hey, Pammy. Not sure. David says if I keep every foal we produce then I'll never break even. It's damn hard letting a baby you've watched be born and grow leave, I will tell you that. I am rather partial to this pair though. I guess only time will tell."

"Yeah. So, are you really going to retire View? I know you're afraid that he will get hurt now that he's getting older, but he's in such great condition... and what will you do? You'll never be happy if you're not competing. The colt you got from Ireland isn't ready, you know that Emmy?"

"Yeah, Pam I know. Well, I was thinking semi-retired. Maybe I'll still take him to dressage and equitation classes, just no more jumping. As far as the colt... Well, no, he's too young and not ready. I'm just going to have to look for another prospect, even if it's one I ride and sell. Otherwise, I can ride and show other people's horses. For example... Are you ready to agree that it's time I take over showing Maverick Destiny for you?"

Pam sighed. Glancing down at her visibly swollen belly, she nodded. "Yeah... David has been pressuring me to surrender the reins to you until after the baby's born. I'm too big to even mount right now anyway. I know he will be in good hands with you. But Emmy he's an Andalusian. He is a dressage horse. He will never fill your void for a Flyer. We need to get you jumping again. It's who you are."

Smiling Emmy said, "I know he is not a jumper. But damn do I love watching that stallion move. He's like poetry in motion. I have two new ones just brought in last week. A Hanoverian colt and a Dutch Warmblood colt. Of the two, the Dutch shows the greatest potential, and the owners want me to show him on the big scale. So I have plenty to keep me busy Pam."

Hearing the insistent whining at her side, Emmy laughed. Looking over her shoulder at the one-hundred-twenty pound, long-haired black and red German shepherd, she crouched down to scratch the dog.

"Besides, Rainy and Feather are keeping me busy. Speaking of Feather, where is that pup?"

Emmy and Pam glanced around the area, looking for the puppy. Hearing a noise around the barn, both women set off with Rainy leading the way. Ahead of them, they could see a small streak of red and white. The women tried to keep their mirth at bay as they watched the four-month-old collie try to herd the six hens into the coop. The hens were not cooperating well.

Laughing, Pam pointed at the pup. "Emmy, you better get that dog a lamb, or she's going to make those hens stop laying eggs if she doesn't learn to leave them be." Pam's laughter died suddenly.

"Oh damn, I need to pee!"

Emmy watched in laughter as her friend waddled as quickly as she could toward the barn bathroom. At nearly seven months pregnant with her first child Pam was radiant. Emmy knew her friend had never been happier. Whistling for the dogs, Emmy walked back around the barn just in time to catch the ringing phone.

Pam came out of the bathroom breathing a sigh of relief. She had never realized a bladder could be so painful until this pregnancy. Watching Emmy on the phone, Pam knew she was in a serious conversation with someone, and most likely about a horse. Catching the sight of a car coming down the drive, Pam sighed. Oh dear, this wasn't going to be good. A year ago David had convinced Emmy to go on a blind date with a friend of his, a man he had personally vouched for and promised Emmy he was an absolute gentleman. Emmy had refused, but eventually, David had worn her down and she agreed to go on one date.

Pam knew this had been an incredibly difficult decision for Emmy. She knew Leo De la Cruz well. He was a very kind man, handsome enough and owned a profitable business. Emmy had liked him enough to give it a try. After six months of dating, however, it became clear Leo wanted a lot more than Emmy.

He wanted what Emmy wasn't ready for. Commitment, and a physical relationship. He just didn't understand that those were two things Emmy couldn't give him yet, maybe never. Emmy had no choice except to end their relationship. For the past six months he had been calling and showing up and refused to give up. Pam knew it was his car making its way toward the barn.

Hanging up the receiver, Emmy walked toward Pam. Watching the approaching car, she said, "Guy on the phone has a crazy horse he wants me to take. Sounds like the horse is more work than it's worth."

Pam glanced at Emmy. Arching a brow, she asked, "Oh yeah? What breed? Does he want you to train it or buy it?"

"An Irish Sport Horse. Supposedly sired by two-time Olympic steeplechaser Celtic Wind, the number one Irish Sport horse in Ireland. Dam is supposed to be Southern Phantom, retired top show jumper. I think I remember the mare. Wasn't she retired right around the time I started my career?"

Pam nodded. "I think so. If I'm thinking of the correct mare, she was a gray, impressive in the show ring. Think it was McDuffie riding her that last year. I think she went to the Olympics a few times too. That sounds like a spectacular eventing prospect. He old enough to start?"

Emmy nodded. "Yeah he's four, which puts him old enough to start beginning competitions, but the guy says the horse is crazy and none of the trainers he's hired have been able to do anything with him. He wants me to take him for a week and if I feel I can work with him he says I can have him for five grand."

Pam's eyes just about popped out of her head. "Five Grand? Are you kidding? That is pennies for those bloodlines. I hope you said yes."

"Yeah. I told him to bring him whenever. Told him I'm not making any promises but I'll take a look. So, you gonna get rid of Leo or I gotta do it?"

Pam grimaced. "Yeah, uh, I think this is your fight, Emmy. You are the one who can't commit. "

Glancing at Pam with an amused expression, she said, "Well, it was your husband who sent him my way, so technically…"

Pam shook her head and giggled as she rushed around and into the barn to see her stallion while Emmy hashed it out with Leo.

Getting out of the car, Leo waved at Emmy. "Hey, Emmy. Look I know I scared you with all that commitment talk, and I'm sorry for that. I'm fine with taking things slow. We can do that. Please, just stop avoiding me."

Emmy closed her eyes in annoyance. "Leo, I'm not avoiding you. I ended our relationship six months ago, and you're not supposed to just keep showing up here. I'm sorry if you didn't want to end things, but we are never going to go anywhere. "

"Damn it, Emmy, why does it have to be this way? Things were good between us, they could have been even better if you wouldn't have been so damn afraid to be physical. To allow commitment in our relationship!"

Emmy blinked in surprise. This was a side of Leo she had not seen before. "Excuse me, you told me you understood if I wanted to forgo any physical relations during our dating. You acted like it wasn't a priority to you. Were you just playing along until you could get down my pants?"

Leo shook his head. "No Emmy, damn it! That's not what I mean. It's just that I wanted us to get married. I wanted to make a life with you, but how am I supposed to do that if you won't even let me touch you?"

Emmy sighed in aggravation. "Yes. Exactly, can't you see that Leo? I cannot be with you physically, I can't marry you. You will never understand any of the reasons. I don't feel that way for you. Even if I wasn't messed up, I wouldn't feel that way, it's just not there. Haven't you noticed that? Haven't you noticed that I am emotionally messed up, Leo?"

Wrapping her arms around herself, Emmy stepped backward. "No Leo, we cannot make this work. We cannot overcome my issues. I have been trying for over nine years. Those events, my past, they will never go away. Leo, I will never be able to make love to you. Never."

Staring hard at her, Leo's brows drew together sharply. "My god, Emmy, what happened to you to make you so afraid?"

Emmy turned away. "I was betrayed by my family, by the people I trusted and looked up to, who I loved. They turned their backs on me when I needed them most. And that's not even the worst part. Now go, Leo. Please just leave and don't come back. This is the last time I am going to tell you not to come here again!" Emmy ran into the barn, trying to hide the tears that stung her eyes. Leo was a good man, and he didn't deserve someone as messed up as her.

Pam pulled Emmy into her arms and held her for several minutes as she wept. All these years that had gone by and the pain was still so raw. Pam was the only part of her childhood she had left. Pam had been her rock, her best friend since she was eight years old. Looking up into the other woman's soulful brown eyes, Emmy whispered, "I love you so much, Pammy."

Pam ran her hand over Emmy's vivid auburn hair. Cooing to her like a child, she said, "And I love you too Emmy. You are the sister of my heart and I will always be here for you. Everything will work itself out in the end ok."

"Let me go you son of a bitch! You get your bloody hands-off me before I box your ears!"

The boy yanked himself out of the older man's grasp before running from the room. Slamming the door behind himself, managing to break the window beside it.

Rae Fitzgerald balled her hands into fists at her side. Turning toward her angry husband, she sent him an angry look. "I told you, Michael, just let him be when he gets like this. You will only make it worse when you get all commanding and authoritative."

Grinding his teeth in anger, Michael Fitzgerald glared at his wife.

"I am not about to back down and let that head-strong teenager treat his parents this way or ruin his life like he's trying to do. He is out of control and you need to stop coddling him, Rae!"

Sighing, Rae realized she would have to face the facts. Her husband was right. He was out of control. Nodding and pulling her husband into her arms, Rae kissed his cheek.

"I know Michael. And I'm sorry. I just did not want to believe it. I think maybe you should call Emmy like you were talking about the other day. Maybe getting him away from the city, and putting him to work on a ranch will help him more than we can. I just feel bad for sending her this burden."

Hanging up the phone Emmy sighed. What was she doing? How could she possibly help Michael and Rea's son when they could barely handle the kid themselves? Emmy was a horse person, not so much a people person. She owed Michael a huge debt, he was the only trainer willing to give her a chance after leaving home and losing her baby. She knew she had to try.

They wouldn't have asked if they hadn't been desperate. Truth be told, Emmy could use a few extra hands around here. If she had more help she would have more time to dedicate to training. Maybe having a teenage boy around wouldn't be so bad.

Glancing down at the two dogs looking adoringly up at her, she sighed, "Well kids, looks like it isn't going to be just the three of us anymore. We've got our work cut out for us, you'll have to help me keep this kid out of trouble while he's here ok." Laughing as the dogs leaped onto her showering her with kisses, Emmy headed off to do her chores.

Shaking his head, Ian Everhart studied the article in front of him. His little sister was all over the magazines again.

"Well, she said she would make something of herself, she said she did not need any of us, and obviously she was right." Ian's eyes took on a distantly remorseful look.

Placing her hand gently on her husband's knee, Miranda sighed as she felt her husband's pain.

"Ian, do you ever wonder about what happened that day outside the track? I know you don't like to talk about it, but I cannot help wondering, would she tell a lie like that to cover up what she had done?"

Sighing, and wiping the tears from his blue eyes, Ian shrugged as he looked into his wife's hazel eyes.

"You know, at first, when it happened I was so certain she had made it up. It wasn't that she had a habit of lying, but she was wild. Besides that, it was no secret how she felt about him. Now, I'm not so sure. Even after she lost... well, even after that she still swore by what she said. All these years and she has stood by what she said."

Taking a deep breath, Ian looked deep into his wife's eyes. "I can't help thinking, would she have left for good if she had been lying? If she was telling us the truth, then we drove our Emmy away when we should have been protecting her."

Feeling her own eyes swell with tears, Miranda looked down at her lap. "I know that if my family had thought I had lied about something like that, and chose a friend over their own child, I would have run faraway and never come back, too. If it's true, then she lost that most sacred part of herself, in a disgusting brutal way, and she lost her baby...because of all of us."

Walking down the aisle of the barn, Emmy smiled when she heard the familiar whinny of her beloved stallion. Coming up to Viewfinder's stall, Emmy stroked the sleek satin neck of the chestnut Holsteiner. This horse was such an important part of her life, if it hadn't been for him she may have never succeeded as she had. You could be an accomplished rider, but without a good horse, you could only get so far. Viewfinder was far more than a good horse.

He was a champion. Sighing, Emmy knew it was going to be hard not to ride him, soaring over the jumps anymore. The stallion nuzzled her face with his soft muzzle. Smiling, Emmy stroked his face.

"You'll be all right, boy. I'm sure spending your days visiting the mares isn't the worst way to go, huh."

Down the aisle, another whinny caught her attention. Smiling, Emmy made her way down the stalls. Stopping to stroke the nearly white face of the Dutch Warmblood colt Olympic Thunder, Emmy smiled. This colt had a lot of promise. The nearly seventeen hand three-year-old colt was all power. He just needed to finish growing out of his goofy stage and he'd be something. Moving down the aisle, Emmy found the gray face she had been looking for.

The young colt still held a youthful look to his face as he studied her with big dark eyes.

"Hey, Shamrock. How are you doing big guy?"

The big gray Colt tossed his head. He was a big stout horse full of power. His name Shamrock Warrior suited the thick-bodied colt well. He was one of the heavyweights here on the ranch. Emmy had first seen the colt when she had been in Ireland three years ago. The colt was only a yearling at the time, but he had caught her eye, and Emmy had seen the promise of a champion in him.

She had bought the colt with two young mares and had them shipped over. His bloodlines were full of champions, and Emmy was truly excited to see the competitor he would make in a few years. Rubbing the stallion's nose, Emmy turned away at the sound of an approaching vehicle.

Emmy watched as Michael's truck came down the long curving drive. They had decided they would leave Greg with her for six months if everything was going well, and go from there. Emmy knew it would be a difficult road ahead of them. The truck stopped near the house, and Michael, Rea, and Greg hopped out and walked toward Emmy.

Hugging Michael and the fiery-haired Rea, Emmy glanced at the sulking Greg. "I hope the drive wasn't too bad. I would have met you guy's part way if I didn't have some mares coming in for breeding today."

"No, it's all right Emmy. You are doing enough for us as it is. I cannot express how grateful we are to ya."

Smiling fondly at Michael and his wife, Emmy stepped toward Greg.

Extending her hand, she said, "Hey there. I'm Emmy. You must be Greg, huh?"

The boy sulked, keeping his eyes downward and refusing to shake her hand. "Yeah. I'm Greg."

Glancing at his parents, Emmy raised a brow. "O.K. well, say your goodbyes and grab your stuff. I'll show you where your room is."

Michael glanced around the beautiful facility. Watching Emmy, he could still remember the day she had come walking onto the farm he was managing, demanding a job. It had been obvious she was a runaway. She'd been skinny, dirty, and the backpack she carried looked like it had seen better days. Despite all this, she had held her chin high and said she'd not take no for an answer. Despite her bravado, it was the sad, lonely and haunted look in the girl's eyes that had made him take pity on her and give her a job mucking stalls.

The day after he'd hired her, Michael had found the poor young woman sleeping in an empty stall, smelly, dirty, and half starved. He'd given the young woman the barn apartment, some food, and sent her to take a shower. He had never regretted his decision as he had watched her work day and night, eventually rising in the ranks. She advanced from stall cleaner and groom, to exercise rider, then to assistant manager, and training assistant.

The young woman had talent. He'd seen few who could ride as well as her, as quietly as her. She had gentle but firm hands and had a special way with horses. Saying goodbye and thanking her again, Michael smiled at the beautiful woman she had become.

Standing beside Emmy as his parents drove away, Greg muttered, "Geez, they really just leave me here, abandon me with a total stranger."

Shrugging, Emmy turned toward the house. "Get used to it kid. That's what families do. They abandon you and cast you away in your time of need. Just the way it is."

Greg frowned as he watched Emmy head toward the house. Picking up his bags, he followed her into the big house. Wandering the whole time what her family had ever done to her to make her say such a thing.

Emmy led Greg to a room on the second floor. Opening the door, she motioned him inside. Greg walked into the room, setting his bags down on the twin sized bed.

"Well, this is your room, Keep it clean, pick up after yourself, and don't make a mess. You will not stay up here sulking in your room all day. You will have your assigned chores and online schooling. Once you finish, you can do as you like."

Frowning at her, Greg knew she was not bluffing. He had the feeling that this woman wouldn't allow him to get away with things the way his mom did.

"Do you know how to cook Greg?" Seeing him shake his head no, Emmy continued.

"You ask me, a boy of fifteen should know how to take care of himself. Anyway, you'll learn. From now on you will be responsible for cooking breakfast twice a week, and dinner twice a week."

Greg gawked at Emmy like she must have sprouted another head. "Are you serious? You really think I'm going to cook? You must be a crazy lady."

Emmy considered him with a look of disdain. "Oh yes, I do. Not only will you cook, but you'll muck stalls, do the dishes, exercise horses, groom, bathe and feed, and pretty much anything else I want you to do."

Seeing the defiant look cross the boy's face, Emmy smiled excessively sweetly.

"Trust me, kid, you won't like the alternative if you decide not to do what I say. You have one hour to settle in, then I will need your help with some breeding's."

Jumping off the bed, Greg said, "You're kidding right? You don't actually expect me to come out there and watch horses have sex do you?"

Emmy laughed at the disgusted look on the kid's face. She almost felt bad for him. "Oh yeah, I do. Don't worry, you can look away if you want to."

Grumbling about horse Sex-Ed, Greg sifted through shavings in the stall he was currently working on. He had only been here a week, and already he'd had to cook, clean, and work in the barn. That didn't even include the breeding sessions she had made him assist with. Gross. Greg was glad there weren't any others around to witness that, it had been embarrassing enough with Emmy there telling him what to do.

He honestly didn't think he was ever going to get that image out of his brain. The first time he'd given Emmy an attitude she had made him scrub rubber mats they did the breeding on. Greg had almost gagged.

Then there was the time he had talked back, and she'd made him scrub the horse trailer inside and out until it shined. With a bloody toothbrush for crying out loud. The woman was loony. At this point, Greg just wanted to go home. Emmy had said the next time he stepped out of line she'd make him sleep in the barn.

He really didn't doubt it. He was not allowed to have headphones, cell phone, or any games. The only time he got to use the computer was when he did online schooling, and Emmy was there hovering watching him the whole time. She'd even hidden the remote to the blasted TV. He was going to lose his mind. He had to admit though, he didn't know how she did all this herself.

The woman woke up when it was dark, and went to bed long after the sun went down. She was like a machine. Three times in the past week, Greg had had to come yell at her to come eat the food he'd made. The other days he had to remind her it was her turn to cook or be forced to feed himself. Finishing the stall, Greg moved his equipment out-of-the-way and closed the stall door.

Hearing the sound of hooves, Greg turned to see Emmy walking up with two saddled horses.

"Care to take a ride, Greg? Your dad said you could ride decent. I could use someone to exercise Bell. I've got my hands full with Oly here. He does better when there's a good solid horse around."

Greg eyed the big bay horse she had called Bell. He knew the big nearly white horse she held onto was Olympic Thunder, a colt she was training for someone. He didn't envy her having to ride the giant. He was all legs and way too much energy. Bell looked much smaller next to the big Warmblood. She stood quietly next to him as the youngster fidgeted and pawed in impatience.

"Come on, she's safe, I promise you. She's one of the lesson horses I use. Really, Greg. I put six-year-olds on her. She's been sitting a lot and I've got lessons coming up soon and she needs to get back in shape. Please."

Eyeing Emmy and the mare, Greg finally shrugged. "Alright. I guess it's better than shoveling horse shi..." Catching the look on Emmy's face he sighed. "Manure."

Emmy watched Greg mount the placid mare. He gathered the reins and glanced at her. Smiling, Emmy turned toward Oly and patted him.

"O.k, Big guy. Let's just take it slow and quiet today. We don't need speed right now, we need coordination."

Greg watched as Emmy gathered the reins in her left hand as she stood on Oly's left side. Slowly, she placed a foot into the stirrup and lifted herself quietly, avoiding pulling on the horse as she did so. As soon as she was in the saddle, Oly tossed his head and blew through his nostrils. Head high the big colt started to rush forward, but Emmy collected him in with a gentle hand and maneuvered him into a large circle instead.

"Go ahead and ride around the arena however you want to Greg. Pretend we are not even here. He just needs the confidence of another horse nearby, that's all."

Greg walked around the arena, feeling the relaxed pace of the mare loosen up his own tense muscles. The mare was easy to ride. Quiet, only needing the softest cue to move along. Watching Emmy put the big rambunctious colt through his circles, half-halts, and starts, reverse arcs, and light trotting, Greg realized she was a remarkable rider. Within the first twenty minutes, the colt began calming down and moving more willingly into the commands from his rider. He was still a bit awkward, trying to come into himself at his young age, but he was a beautiful animal.

Forty minutes later, Emmy and Greg were removing the tack from their mounts when the sound of a truck and trailer came down the drive. The sounds of a horse kicking the sides of the trailer were easy enough to hear. Glancing at Emmy, Greg asked, "You expecting more mares?"

Laughing at the grimace on Greg's face, Emmy shook her head. "Nope, not this week. I'm going to guess by all the kicking that's the crazy horse someone wants me to work with."

Greg frowned. "Crazy horse? Surely you wouldn't work with something that would be dangerous right?"

Smiling, Emmy shrugged. "All horses can be dangerous, Greg. All it takes is the right circumstances and someone who's not paying enough attention. It's all part of the game. You play with horses you run the risk of getting hurt. Especially trainers and competitors."

The truck pulled to a halt, and an older man with graying hair hopped out. Walking toward Emmy and Greg, he called, "You Ms. Everhart?"

When Emmy nodded, he continued, "Ah, well thanks for agreeing to give him a try. I won't blame you if you end up wanting no part of him though. Where would you like me to unload him? I would suggest not to put him in a stall or anywhere too confined, but I also wouldn't put him anywhere big enough to get the momentum to jump out."

Arching an auburn brow, Emmy's attention was not fully on the man.

"Oh? Has he jumped out of pens before?"

Nodding the man sighed. "Yeah. We tried stalling him, he only got meaner. We put him in a small pasture with four-foot fences, and he cleared those without a thought. We've been keeping him in an enclosed round pen lately."

Emmy frowned. "Well, maybe one of the smaller paddocks then. All my fences here are five-foot tall, and all have a second fence around them. We breed and train jumpers, so we prepared for that when we built the place."

The man nodded. "That's good, I think he'd be okay in a paddock. I'll back the trailer up and we'll let him jump out, just point me in the direction."

Emmy and Greg stood near the gate and watched as the man opened the trailer door at the opening to the paddock. Soon as the door was open, the horse flew from the trailer, quickly rushing the fence lines. The man quickly pulled the gate closed and latched it.

"You got any chains around here? He knows how to open just about any barn or fence latch."

Emmy laughed as she watched the animal in front of her. He was truly something to behold. With a large powerful build, the colt must have been at least sixteen-two hands, and close to twelve hundred pounds. He was massive but athletic. His coat was mostly black, but small areas were starting to gray with vivid deep blue-gray dapples on his shoulders and flanks. The colt had a long mane and tail and a forelock that reached halfway down his face. Long graceful legs and a powerful but finely chiseled face made the horse exceptionally beautiful.

Emmy stared in awe. The colt ran, spun, kicked, bucked, reared, and thrashed around the paddock testing every inch of the fence line. Finally halting in front of the shelter, the stallion blew air out of his nostrils in a powerful burst. Emmy glanced at the old man. "Wow. That is an incredibly impressive horse, Mr..."

"Mr. Geraldo. Sam Geraldo. Yes, impressive to look at is right. You should see his pedigree. The damn horse should be worth a small fortune, but he's tried to kill every trainer I've taken him to."

Emmy frowned. "Tell me, Mr. Geraldo, did somthing happen to him to cause him to mistrust humans, or was he just born with a bad temperament?"

Sighing, Sam said, "Nothing's ever happened to him to cause any kind of fear that I know of. He was a feisty but friendly foal. He never displayed signs of foul temperament, but he was out with the other mares and foals on the property till he was about two. When we tried to start working with him, it was like he'd gone wild. He's the only one outta the whole bunch that came back this way."

Emmy stood watching the horse for many hours after Mr. Geraldo had gone. Something about the horse called out to her soul, almost as though a piece of him was broken just as a piece of her was. He was an exceptional animal. One of the most amazing horses she had ever seen. There was no doubt that his pedigree was top of the line.

It was, however, his eyes that held her attention the most. They held a wild look. A need to flee that made everything else around him unimportant. She watched him, and he watched her. Every movement she made caused a reaction from him. She tilted her head, and the horse flattened his ears. She lifted a shoulder, and his haunches tensed, ready to run. She took a deep breath, and he'd blow air out his nostrils aggressively.

The colt was hyperaware of everything around him, and Emmy saw the potential he had to be a great. She didn't see a crazy animal that wanted to hurt someone. She saw an animal that felt trapped, scared, and unsure of himself. He would hurt her if he must, but Emmy didn't believe he would do it because he was mean. His eyes watched her with an intelligence not often found. He was watching, waiting, and analyzing this new situation.

Greg walked up slowly behind Emmy. They had finished the chores and feeding hours ago, and dinner had been sitting a while. He'd peered out of the house several times to find Emmy always here in the same spot, watching the horse. He didn't know why she seemed so entrapped by this horse, but Greg approached slowly, almost as though he was approaching two wild animals. He didn't want to startle her or the horse.

Calling softly, he said, "Emmy, uh, dinner's been ready for a while now, you going to come inside?"

Emmy glanced at Greg, seemingly coming out of her trance. Nodding she cleared her throat and looked away, suddenly aware of the tears that had begun sliding down her cheeks unbidden.

"Yeah, thanks, Greg. I'll be right there."

As he watched, Greg noticed Emmy take two sugar cubes from her pocket and leave them on top of the fence where she'd been standing. He didn't know why she was crying, but he knew it was best to leave it alone.

For the next several days, Emmy left the colt by himself. He still ran the fence line and tensed whenever she or Greg would approach. So far, the colt had not tried to jump the fences, for which Emmy was grateful. After a few days, Emmy began entering the paddock when feeding the colt. At first, the colt's reaction was to stomp the ground in aggression, but after a few days of this, he began to stand quietly and watch her. She filled the bucket and put hay into the feeder, ignoring the colt the whole time.

After the colt had been there for six days, Emmy was leading one of her mares into a nearby pasture when she heard Greg calling out from the barn. Emmy turned toward the barn where she heard Greg, but at that second a flash of movement to her left caught her attention. In the paddock a few hundred feet away, the colt was rearing and thrashing wildly. Frowning, Emmy couldn't imagine what had the horse so worked up now. Releasing the mare into the two-acre turnout, Emmy closed the gate and headed toward the colt. As she neared his paddock, the horse stood eerily still in the back corner, head held high, ears flicking and looking straight ahead.

Emmy had a bad feeling right away. Sure enough, just as she reached the gate to his paddock, the colt launched himself forward and ran full speed toward the opposite fence. In three long strides, the stallion had reached the end of the paddock. Shoving off with his hindquarters, the colt flew up and over the five-foot fence with easily a foot to spare.

Emmy's heart just about stopped as the horse landed, took one long stride, and launched himself over the next five-foot fence. The alley that separated the paddock from one of the large pastures was only about twenty feet wide. Not very many horses would have taken two five-foot fences in such close succession so easily. Emmy was impressed. Watching the stallion gallop and buck through the large pasture, Emmy realized what had set him off. He was headed straight toward her Irish Draught mare.

Up and over the next two fences he went, and before Emmy could even get halfway there, the colt was in the pasture with her chestnut mare. Emmy ran to the gate, praying the two would not fight. She knew the mare was not in heat, so she didn't think that to be the reason the colt went to her. As she neared the gate, the two horses circled each other, squealed a few times, and the big colt reared a couple feet in the air. Then, as if the pair had been long lost companions, the mare went back to her grazing, and the colt stood docilely by her side.

Stopping at the fence, Emmy watched in surprise. Finally, after several minutes, Emmy was convinced the colt had just wanted the companionship of another horse. Emmy also realized that if these two were going to bond, she could use that to her advantage. Fiorghr'a was a sweet six-year-old mare who adored people. She came to the gate anytime someone approached and strived on human attention. Maybe through the mare, Emmy might be able to gain the colt's trust.

Testing her theory, Emmy called to the mare, who lifted her head and nickered softly. Seeing Emmy approaching the gate, the mare happily trotted over to her. The colt, Emmy was amused to note, was upset by this odd behavior. Tossing his head and letting out a high-pitched whinny, he began pawing the ground in agitation. The mare ignored her new friend, content to lean into the fence as Emmy scratched her shoulder.

When Emmy reached into her pocket, the mare nickered happily and snatched the sugar cubes up. Seeing this interaction, the colt perked his ears and took a few tentative steps forward. Emmy knew he wouldn't come to her, but it was a step in the right decision. Having made up her mind, she headed toward the barn.

As Emmy approached Greg ran up to her. "Oh my gosh, Emmy, did you see that bloody horse clear those fences? I've never seen anything like that. What made him go over there like that anyway?"

Emmy smiled, remembering the colt's focus right before he took off toward that first fence.

"Yes, he is quite something, isn't he? Very few horses, especially untrained ones would've made two consecutive jumps so close together like that. You know, taking Fiorgrh'a out today, I didn't even think about the fact that she was the first horse I was turning out since he's been here. The others have been in the barn this whole week, maybe he was just tired of being alone. I don't think it will hurt anything for them to be together as long as they are getting along."

Picking up the phone in the barn, Emmy looked at the card she had tacked to the whiteboard and dialed. After a few rings, Sam Geraldo picked up.

"Hello, this is Sam."

"Hi, Sam, this is Emmy Everhart. I have that Irish Sport colt of yours, remember?" Emmy waited for him to reply.

"Oh, yeah, I remember Miss Everhart. Let me guess? He's destroyed your farm and tried to kill you and you want me to come get him right this second, right?"

Laughing, Emmy said, "No, no Sam, nothing of the sort. Well, he did clear the fences of that paddock, but it's fine now. Actually, I was calling because I want to accept your offer. I want to buy him."

There was a long pause at the other end. "Well... I have to say, I didn't see this coming. Were you able to catch him?"

"No, I actually haven't even tried to lay a hand on him at all. Closest I've come was walking into the pen and putting hay in the feeder. I've been giving him space and observing him. I think it will take a lot longer than most horses to bring him around, but I think he's worth it. So, do we have a deal?"

Sam chuckled. "You're a brave soul, Miss Everhart. No one here would've dared feed him inside his pen. The fact that he let you go in there and didn't go after you speaks volumes in itself. You have a deal. I will keep my word. Since you're on the phone, I got a question for you, Miss Everhart."

Emmy nodded into the receiver. "Sure Sam, ask away. I would be happy to help you with anything I can."

"Well, Miss Everhart, My trainer quit on me, and I got six youngsters I need started and four show horses I need ridden and shown. I'd be willing to take you on as a new trainer and make a contract with you if you would be willing. You'll probably cost me a lot more than my last trainer, but I got good horses and they need to be shown for what they are. What's the point in breeding if they never make it to the ring?"

Emmy grinned from ear to ear. This day had just gotten better. "I would be thrilled to take on the contract as your trainer Sam. If your other horses are anything like this colt, then they definitely need to be shown. Just let me know when you want to bring the ten over."

Hanging up the phone, Emmy turned to Greg and grinned broadly. "Well Greg, I guess we're going to have to get you some help. We just got our first real training contract!" Pulling him into a strangling hug, Emmy jumped up and down.

Greg wasn't sure what to do at first. He wanted to act hard and tough, but the truth was he had come to greatly like and care about this crazy woman greatly in the weeks' time he had been there.

When she finally released him, he said, "Yeah, ain't no way I'm gonna be able to keep up on everything myself. And you're gonna be too busy riding horses to help, but I'll tell you what, I'm not cooking for anyone else, got it."

Emmy laughed at Greg. "Yeah kid, I got it. I got it. You're going to have to help me exercise more than just Bell though."

-5-

Westley drove down the long winding tree-lined driveway for the second time in his life. As he rounded the bend in the road, the house and barn came into view and Westley whistled at all the changes they had made in the past few years. The house had been painted a delicate powder blue with white trims, flowers decorated the entire perimeter as well as a nicely manicured green lawn that wrapped around the house.

In addition to the barn that was already there, the property now boasted a huge barn that Westley figured must hold at least forty stalls. An indoor arena, outdoor arena, and several shelters and paddocks had also been added to the property. As he pulled up toward the barn, he could see a couple of people on horses and a few standing at the fence. Even though it probably wasn't the best time to come by, he figured she was less likely to throw him out if there were others around.

Parking, Westley headed toward the arena. Instantly realizing Emmy was one of the people on horseback, he took a seat on the bleachers to wait.

A woman approached him shortly after. Smiling flirtatiously, she asked, "You here for lessons sweetheart?"

Westley groaned silently. He really didn't have the patience to deal with this type of woman today. "Uh, yeah, something like that. You?"

The woman nodded her blond head. "Yep. My daughter and I have been taking lessons from Emmy for the past few weeks, and I must say, she's the best instructor we've had so far. I doubt I'll be able to ride as well as her, but my daughter's young and has lots of time to learn."

Westley nodded. "Yes, the younger they start, the better. Who are the others out there? Other students?"

Shaking her head, the woman said, "Oh, no, Emmy doesn't do group lessons. Says there is no way she could really give them her undivided attention if she has too many students at a time. The most she will do at a time is two, for people who are coming together you know. It's one of the things we like about her. I believe one of them is interviewing for a position, and the other is someone who helps her maybe. Guess she's getting busier, and can't do it alone anymore."

Westley turned his attention back to the riders. One of the girls looked like an intermediate rider, while it was easy to tell the other was a novice rider, with little interest. The third rider was a young man who seemed a little under confident but was using all the right cues. Finally, all four riders stopped before dismounting.

"All right, good job Abby. Keep practicing at home, I can see that you are improving, we just need to get you a little more focused and then we can talk about entering some small shows, ok."

At this, the little blond girl perked up and nodded excitably. Jogging to her mother, she bounced up and down. The woman looked up as Emmy approached.

"Hey, Emmy, would it be too much to ask if you can take care of Blue for us today? We have an appointment we need to get to."

Emmy shrugged, but Westley could see the irritation in the movement. "Yeah, sure Jeannette, but next time try to leave enough time in your schedule to take care of Blue. He is Abby's horse, and the responsibility of taking care of him is just as important as riding."

The woman nodded, smiling sweetly, and said goodbye. Emmy shook her head.

"Woman's a pain in the..." Glancing sideways, Emmy's gaze met that of a man approaching her. When the realization hit her that it was Westley who stood there, Emmy wanted to scream. She so did not have time for the one man who both drove her crazy and stirred her attraction.

Turning away from him, she strode toward the other people leading horses out of the arena. Grabbing the discarded reins of the big flea-bitten gelding, Emmy whirled back around and caught Westley by surprise.

Offering the reins to him, she said, "Westley Galway, I don't know what you want, or why you've come, but if you're going to make a nuisance of yourself you might as well be useful."

As Emmy turned away from him, Westley couldn't stop the wide grin that came to his mouth. She had not been happy to see him, but the reaction he had received hadn't been at all what he had expected. Leading the gelding into the large barn, Westley understood why. The barn had at least fifteen horses in their stalls, and Westley had seen several more out in the pastures and turnouts. It was no wonder she needed the extra help. As he began unsaddling the quiet gelding, Westley listened closely as Emmy spoke to the young woman behind him.

"Well, I like the way you ride Michelle. There's no doubt you've taken lessons. I need someone with your skill. There are many trainees and just as many horses that need exercising and showing. My partner Pam will be out for the rest of the season, and part of next season as well. She comes and helps with lessons a couple times a week, but that's about the most she can do right now."

The young woman looked up at Emmy then. "Well, Miss Everhart, I'd be happy to help exercise, clean stalls, help with lessons, and even show, or anything you need me to do. Unfortunately, I'm afraid I've no experience at all with colts, stallions, or starting an inexperienced horse."

Westley studied the young woman, who he figured to be around seventeen or eighteen. He watched Emmy frown, as she struggled to decide, and he could see she needed the help. She had a lot on her plate here running this place, training and showing other people's horses, and clearly, she still needed time to train her own. That's when it hit him. It was the perfect excuse for why he was here, and a perfect excuse to keep seeing her, to keep being around. It was all he'd thought about for the past three years.

Clearing his throat, Westley grinned at Emmy. "Well, that actually works out quite well for me then, seeing as how I came here hoping to land a job training and starting colts."

Emmy's head whipped around, and she glared daggers at him. "You cannot be serious?" Seeing that he clearly was, Emmy closed her eyes, counted to five, took a deep breath, and turned back to the young woman.

"Michelle, I'd be happy to take you on. You would be a huge help to me even without starting colts. I know you're going to be starting college this fall, so for now, I'm willing to give you full-time, Tuesday through Saturday if that works with you?"

Michelle's face brightened up. "Oh, Miss Everhart, that would be perfect, you don't know what that would mean to me. Since we moved here I haven't even been near a horse, oh thank you so much."

Emmy smiled. "You're welcome. We will be happy to have the help. When you start classes we will adjust your schedule as needed. We will see you tomorrow at seven am okay?"

Nodding her head enthusiastically, Michelle headed toward her car.

Walking up behind Emmy, Greg sighed, "Ahh, come on Em, you let her off easy, you could have at least let her help unsaddle and put away. Now I've got twice as much work to do."

Sighing back at him, Emmy looked over at Greg. It had been a long day and she knew he was tired. A thought came to mind, and Emmy smiled wickedly.

"Oh, it's all right Greg. Why don't you go on up to the house, shower and relax, Mr. Galway here has a working interview to do, so he'll help me finish the night's chores."

Greg glanced from one to the other of them. He didn't know who this guy was, but he could nearly cut the tension between the two with a knife. Nodding he backed away.

Pointing toward Rainy, he said, "You stay with Emmy. Good girl."

Westley grinned. Emmy thought she had just pulled a fast one on him, but what she didn't know was that he would be all too happy to help her.

Smiling over at her, he said, "So, Boss, where would you like me to start?"

Emmy's deep blue eyes glared at Westley. "You're not hired. Help me finish putting these horses away. That's Blue."

Turning to point to the bay tied up on the next cross tie, she said, "And that's Bell. You can unsaddle those two and after they are properly rubbed down, put them away. They all have nameplates on their stalls."

Turning, Emmy continued to take the tack off the sorrel mare she had been riding. What was he doing here? Why would he show up at her farm out of the blue after nearly three years? What's worse, why did she still feel all those odd feelings whenever he was around, like her body and mind where hyperaware of him? This was ridiculous. Maybe she hadn't forgotten about him and her attraction to him in the past three years, but she sure in the hell never expected to see him again.

Westley whistled an Irish tune as he curried down the flea-bitten gray gelding called Blue. "So this guy belongs to your student, huh? I didn't know you did boarding here as well."

Emmy shook her head. "I don't. I only do boarding for student horses. No outside boarders. It makes lessons a lot easier if they have their own horse here to train on, that way I can see all the issues that need working on. Many times the horse needs work too. Blue there, however, is perfect. If only his rider would take a little more interest."

Westley nodded. Leading the finished Blue to his stall, he scanned the horses and names as he passed them. Several good-looking horses eyed him as he passed. Walking back toward Bell once old Blue was resting happily, Westley frowned.

"I don't see Viewfinder in here? Is he still here?"

Emmy nodded toward the smaller barn that stood about a hundred yards away. "He stays in my personal barn with a few others. I'm thinking about either expanding it or building another one. I like having my horses separate from the others. Especially the stallions."

Once all the horses had been taken care of and put away, Emmy led Westley to the ATV they used for feeding. The trailer attached was filled with hay and buckets of grain already. "Lucky for you we have started keeping some of the horses out because the weather's warmed up and there is plenty of grass now."

Westley smiled. She was so damn beautiful. Her deep auburn hair was pulled back into a long braid that hung down to just above her hips, and her jeans hugged her figure just right. Glancing up to see Emmy watching him with an exasperated expression, Westley grinned. He couldn't help himself.

"Are you quite done with ogling me, Mr. Galway?" Emmy was mad. She hated when men looked at her like that. Mostly she was angry with the way her skin burned everywhere his eyes had roved, and angry at her mind for giving her images of his hands following those same paths. She didn't understand these feelings he evoked when all other men had made her feel dirty, disgusted, and even scared.

Westley's grin only broadened. "Yeah. I'm sorry Emmy, It's just that you are so damn beautiful. I cannot help myself. I guess I shouldn't say things like that to my boss though huh?"

Emmy groaned. This man was vexing. "Westley, you're not here to get a job, and even if you were I'd not be giving you one so you can stop the act already."

Glancing at Emmy, Westley shook his head.

"I was serious Emmy. I've just recently come back to the States, and I could use a job. I'm still staying in a motel. I was hoping you'd have a live-in position available. I can do anything you need me to. I'm experienced with training and starting colts, I have breeding and foaling experience, and I can fix just about anything. I'm just the person you need around here, and you know it, Emmy."

Sighing, Emmy still wasn't sure Westley actually needed a job here. He did have a point though. She did need someone like him around the farm. She didn't know how much experience he had, or how good he was, but she didn't have anyone else with such skills knocking at her door.

"The problem is, Westley, even if I wanted to hire you, I don't have a barn apartment for you to stay in, and

I'm not sure I feel comfortable letting you stay in my house."

Westley knew there was one sure way to change her mind. He didn't know what it was about this woman, but he desperately wanted to be a part of her life. God knew he didn't need the money, the job, or a place to stay. He had plenty of money on his own. Getting back into the horse world had not been his plan, but after his family announced their decision to sell most of the farm, and horses, he had little choice.

He didn't know where he wanted to be or what he wanted to do. The only thing he had known with certainty these last three years was that the feelings between Emmy and him were not going away. There was an invisible connection, and he knew he wanted to be with her. If only she would just give him the chance.

"Put me on a horse Emmy. You know you need me, but I can still see the doubt in your eyes. I understand you don't know me that well, and you know almost nothing about my life with horses. Put me on a horse. Any horse. Any level, and you'll no more have any doubts."

Emmy almost smiled at the confidence he exuded. She did smile at the end of his sentence when his Irish brogue started to slip out. "Ok. Fine. Any horse, you say?"

At Westley's nod, Emmy racked her brain to think of the horse that would test him and best show her what his skills were.

Smiling mischievously, Emmy said, "Come on, I have just the horse."

Westley studied the sixteen hand black mare that Emmy pulled from the stall. The nameplate read Ru'ndaingne. Lifting his brow, he asked, "Strong willed, huh? That's an interesting name to give a horse. Where'd you pick this one up?"

Grinning despite her struggle to dislike him, she found Westley to be freshly different from most men she had met. He seemed so confident, so down-to-earth and laid-back about everything. As much as she hated to admit it, she found him charming.

"Three years ago, after our last meeting in Ireland, I bought several horses from a breeding farm there. She was a two-year-old then, and I liked her spirit. I bought her and two others. A colt and a broodmare in foal. She is getting much closer to being ready to show, but we've got some work to do yet."

Once saddled, Emmy led Westley and Ru toward the indoor arena. When they entered the large oval-shaped space, he saw why. This was the jumping arena.

Turning toward Westley, Emmy said, "I'd like to see you ride perimeter in dressage style first as you warm her up. After that I want to see how the two of you handle some small single and double Oxers."

Adjusting the saddle to his settings, Westley shrugged. "No problem. Anything else you'd like to see? Flying over the moon perhaps or a bow or two?"

Emmy shot him an exasperated look. "Just go ride the damn horse Westley before your mouth gets you into trouble."

As he mounted and nudged the horse forward, Westley grinned wickedly. Oh, he could think of a few ways to get his mouth into trouble with Emmy all right.

The look on Westley's face was not lost on Emmy as she posted herself near the doorway. A shiver ran down her spine as her mind provided her with a few unwanted images. Shrugging it off Emmy stood firm. She would not let this man get to her. She knew exactly what men all wanted deep down, and she was so never allowing that to happen to her again.

Westley casually walked the mare around the perimeter as he allowed them to get the feel of each other. The mare was bold, fairly soft mouthed, with a big, confident stride. He had to admit she felt good. This horse would make an excellent competitor. He could almost sense the mare's anticipation as he asked her to pick up a soft trot. Through the walk, trot, and canter around the arena, the mare tried several times to anticipate Westley's command before he actually followed through with giving it. This could be an advantage, or it could be a disaster when jumping.

Bringing the mare into a reverse arc across the center of the arena, Westley could feel the mare's gaze consistently stray toward the jumps. She was definitely a jumper. When he had warmed her up through a few light diagonals, and half passes, Westley asked her for the first jump, and nearly lost his seat. The mare took the two-foot jump like a five-footer. Pulling her to a halt, he repositioned himself and began again.

This time he expected the big leap and pulled the mare up into a slower more collected stride before the jump. The mare responded well. The jump was a four-footer instead of a five-footer this time. Not perfect, but an improvement. It wasn't a bad thing that the mare wanted to jump big, but Westley wanted the mare's attention focused on him.

Emmy watched Westley from her spot by the door. She giggled at the surprise on his face at the first big jump. After that, Emmy watched as Westley went through jump after jump with the mare, constantly correcting her. The mare fought him at first but after a while, she complied and followed his cues. He was incredible. Emmy realized he could well be a better rider than her. How had he kept this gift hidden? The longer she watched him, the more her admiration for him grew.

Westley pulled the mare up in front of Emmy after cooling her out. Patting her neck, he looked up at Emmy to find her watching him with a look of utter admiration in her big blue eyes.

"This mare is really something, Emmy. The fire and drive she has for jumping will take her far."

Emmy smiled. "Yes, she is undoubtedly one of my best prospects. And significantly better than any of my trainees, so far. I got really lucky with her. You looked pretty damn good up there, Westley. I had no idea you could ride so well. You belong in the show ring."

Looking down into Emmy's eyes, Westley had to resist the urge to pull her into his arms and kiss that beautiful smile. Instead, he dismounted and said gently, but firmly, "No. I will do anything else you ask of me, but I will not show."

Emmy couldn't hide the surprise on her face. Grabbing Westley's arm to make him face her, she said, "But, Westley, how can you not show? You are better than I am! Surely you realize that."

Westley looked down where Emmy's hand lay firmly on his arm. Taking a deep breath to still the hunger her mere touch elicited, Westley shook his head.

"No, Emmy. I am not better than you. I am good, but you are the best. There is a reason they say you "Fly" over the jumps. Your movements are so subtle, so perfect. You're always in sync with your mount. You are truly an inspirational rider. I cannot and will not show. That is my one condition, but I will help you train."

Emmy studied Westley before quickly removing her hand. She had felt the sudden heat the innocent gesture brought to the pit of her stomach, and she had seen the hunger that ignited in his eyes. This man was very dangerous to her. There was no doubt about that. There was, unfortunately, also no doubt that she needed his help at the ranch.

"All right, Westley. You can have the job, and I'll give you the downstairs room in the house. It has its own bathroom. We can discuss pay later. I won't push you to show anymore."

Westley smiled broadly. "Thank you. I do have a condition though. I will take little to no pay if you will allow me to bring my horses here. My family decided to sell most of the farm back home, and I couldn't let them go. Those bloodlines have been in my family for generations. We prided ourselves on having the best horse stock in all Ireland. I took the best we had as my share in the ranch, but now I'll be needing somewhere to keep them. I was thinking you might be willing to show them for me in exchange for a portion of the profits from any winnings or sales?"

Emmy was a little taken back. She hadn't been expecting this at all. "Well now, I hadn't seen that one coming. How many horses will you be needing to bring?"

Westley smiled sheepishly. "Well, I have two stallions, six mares in foal, and four between the ages of two and six."

Emmy swallowed. She hadn't expected so many horses. Her barn still had a lot of space, and if they mostly went out in the larger pasture it wouldn't put much strain on her.

"Well, I have the room. Are they Irish Draughts?"

Westley shook his head no. "Not all. Some, the studs are approved Irish Warmbloods, and a few of the mares as well. Every single one of them has champion bloodlines that have been in my family for more than four generations. I couldn't let the Galway legacy end and these horses end up with just anyone. I plan to continue their bloodlines, even if I have to do it here in America."

Shaking her head, Emmy said, "It's not a problem, Westley. You can bring them here and we can work something out. Don't worry. I have to ask though, you're so passionate when you speak of Ireland, why didn't you stay and start over there?"

Westley studied Emmy for a long time. He could see the compassion in her eyes as he had told her about his family selling the farm. The more time he spent with her, the more he liked her. It wasn't just her beauty either. It was her spirit, her fire, her stubbornness, and the kindness he could see there, no matter how hard she tried to fight it.

"There was something here in America I wanted more."

Without giving any detail to that cryptic comment, Westley turned and began taking care of the mare. Emmy struggled to understand what he could possibly want here in America more than he wanted to be in Ireland with his history, and homeland.

Once all the chores had been taken care of, Emmy turned to Westley, "Would you like to have dinner with us, Mr. Galway? You've helped me a lot tonight and I really appreciate it."

Grinning, Westley said, "I'd love to Ms. Everhart. And you're the one doing me a huge favor letting me bring my horses here."

Inside, Emmy smiled to herself as she smelled the delicious aromas coming from the kitchen. Greg may have griped about having to learn how to cook, but he had completely embraced it. Tonight was actually her night to cook.

"Hey kid, you know no one's going to believe you don't like cooking if you keep volunteering on my nights."

Greg stuck his head around the corner and grinned. "Well, we'd all starve if we were forced to eat your cooking all the time!"

Emmy's jaw dropped. "Why you little monster! I can't be that bad a chef if I taught you how to cook and you're still alive."

Greg was about to retort when he saw the man standing slightly behind Emmy.

Wiping his hands, he stepped forward and held out his hand. "Hi, I'm Greg Fitzgerald."

Glancing from the teenage kid to Emmy, Westley wondered what their relationship was.

"I'm Westley Galway. Nice to meet you. Your cooking smells great."

Cocking a sandy colored brow, Greg said, "Thanks. Is that an Irish accent I detect Mr. Galway?"

Grinning, Westley nodded. "Aye. Born and raised. I'm guessing with a name like Fitzgerald you've got at least a touch as well."

"Yep. My dad's full, moms half Scottish. Kinda funny hearing them tear into each other when they get mad."

Westley laughed. "Irish and Scottish, eh? Well you must be a pretty stubborn bloke when you want to be, huh?"

Greg grinned back at him. "Sure the hell, can be bloody stubborn when I want to be man, if you know what I mean."

Greg winced at the look on Emmy's face. "Ah, come on Em, it wasn't even a bad curse word. Don't make me scrub that breeding mat again!"

Emmy laughed. "All right, just this once I will let you off the hook, but next time you curse I'm going to make you do worse than scrubbing that mat, you hear?"

Turning to Westley, Emmy said, "Please make yourself comfortable, I'm going to go clean up a bit."

Westley walked into the large open living room. The house was very nice. It had original, restored hardwood floors, tall ceilings, and lots of charm. All the furniture had a western feel to it, with many wood accents. Westley noticed there weren't any pictures of family on the wall like you'd expect.

Seeing the large fireplace in the center of one wall, Westley caught sight of a framed photo of two young women in their early teens. It was obvious one was Emmy, although her hair was a bit brighter shade of red then. The other young woman had darker skin, dark hair and big brown eyes. He guessed that must be Pam Ryans.

Smiling at the pair seated together on a big chestnut horse, clearly in love with life, Westley couldn't help thinking Emmy was a lovely child. Such fire in her eyes even then. Noticing a smaller photo next to that picture, Westley picked it up and studied it. At first, he had thought it might be a picture of Emmy as a baby, but reading the words written across the top, he realized it wasn't.

Grace Everhart: June 16, 1998-June 18, 1998. The baby was wrapped in a delicate pink blanket, and it was clear she was very small and delicate. The dates showed she had only lived for two days.

Walking into the room, Emmy found Westley studying the picture of pale sweet Grace. Clearing her throat, Emmy crossed the room to stand beside Westley. Taking the picture from him, Emmy felt her composure slip.

"She was my miracle. My very own little miracle. She was born three months too early. The doctors did everything they could for her, but she was so frail. They didn't think she would make it through that first night, but she gave me two wonderful days."

Studying Emmy's tear-filled gaze, Westley felt his heartbreak for her. He couldn't imagine what it felt like to lose a child.

"I didn't know you had any children."

Nodding, Emmy said, "She wasn't meant to be. She was never meant to have been conceived, but I loved her anyway. I loved her so much."

Westley clenched his jaw. He wanted so bad to pull her into his arms and offer her comfort, but he knew it would not be welcomed. "What of the Father?"

Suddenly, Emmy's eyes turn cold and hard. She had put the walls back up. Emmy moved away from Westley. Placing the picture delicately back on the mantel before turning toward the kitchen. "I believe the food is ready, Mr. Galway."

Westley sighed. He'd asked the wrong question and now she had shut herself off to him again. He didn't know what the story was with the man who had gotten her pregnant, but it obviously wasn't something she was willing to talk about. He wouldn't have thought of Emmy as someone who'd had a baby. Doing the math in his head, he realized that based on how old he guessed her to be, she must have been young at the time. It was no wonder she refused to trust anyone.

Greg served dinner. Spaghetti with meatballs and salad. It was delicious. For a fifteen-year-old, the kid knew how to cook. Glancing at Greg, Westley commented on the dinner. "Man, Greg, this is great. Maybe you should go to culinary school."

Greg smiled at the compliment. "Thanks, Westley. Actually, I've been thinking about it. When Emmy first made me learn to cook, I was pretty annoyed. But, now that I've been learning, I find I like it."

Glancing at Emmy, Greg continued, "Hey Em, I found this perfect Scottish dish I want to try for my mom when she and Dad come for a visit. Hope you don't mind, but that means you'll have to be my guinea pig."

Emmy smiled. "I know your mom is going to be absolutely shocked at the change in you, Greg. Especially if you cook her a meal like that. She will be really proud of you."

Greg swallowed and looked down at the table. "Yeah. I was a real weasel to them. I feel really bad for how I was acting. I miss them, ya know, but Em, I would like to keep staying here if that's cool with you? At least for the time, we had agreed on. I don't really like the city and though I miss Mom and Dad, I don't want to go back yet."

Emmy smiled lovingly at Greg. The kid had grown on her. Even though the first couple weeks had been a little tough, deep down he was a good kid, with a good heart.

"Of course Greg. I'm sure your parents will agree that this place has been good for you. Besides, they promised me a slave for six months, and I plan to cash in on that."

Winking at Greg, she continued, "Well, Greg, the good news is you'll have extra help now, and another guinea pig. Mr. Galway will be taking a job here, and staying in the downstairs bedroom."

Frowning, Greg glanced from Emmy to Westley. He wasn't sure how he felt about this guy moving in. He might be just a teenager, but he knew enough to know the way Westley looked at Emmy meant he was attracted to her. The man could barely keep his eyes off her.

"Oh, wow. Well, uh, are you sure that's a good idea Em? No offense Mr. Galway, but you're a guy and all and well I don't know exactly what you want with Emmy…"

Laughing, Emmy glanced at Greg. "Really, Greg, it is ok. Mr. Galway and I are not strangers. We've met a few times before, and I appreciate the protectiveness, but I think it will be ok. We could use his help, too."

Greg shrugged. "Emmy, have you ever been married?" Greg watched Emmy choke on her drink. "Sorry, just curious."

Glancing at Greg, and wondering where in the world this had come from, Emmy looked down at her plate. "No, Greg, I've never been married. I can't say it's something I plan to ever do either."

Frowning, Greg asked, "Well, you may not plan it, but you would if the right person came along, right? I mean, falling in love and getting married isn't something we plan out right?"

Emmy sighed. "I don't know, Greg. I've never been in love, never really expecting to, and I am not expecting to get married. I am afraid not everyone is meant for love and marriage."

The buzzing of the telephone saved Emmy from playing anymore fifty questions with Greg, and for that she was thankful. Picking up the receiver, Emmy answered. "Hello?"

The voice on the other end was familiar but unwelcome. "Emmy? Emmy, it's me, Miranda. Please, don't hang up. Something terrible has happened."

Emmy's lips drew into a thin line. Thousands of thoughts raced through her mind. "I'm listening, Miranda."

"All right. You need to come down here right away. It's Ian. He's been in a car accident. He's at the hospital here in town, you know the one. Please, I know you hate him, but they don't know if he's going to make it, and all he does is ask for you."

Emmy could hear the tears and despair in Miranda's voice. "All right, Miranda, I'll be there as soon as I can."

Hanging up the receiver, Emmy turned toward Greg and Westley. "I'm afraid I have to go. There's been an emergency."

Westley had noticed the moment Emmy's face had drained of all color. She grabbed her purse and keys from the counter and ran outside. Westley jumped up to run after her, followed closely by Greg.

"She's too upset to drive herself."

Emmy had just inserted the key into the truck's ignition after the fifth try. Her hands were shaking so badly, she could barely get the darn key turned. Her door wrenched open, and Westley stood there.

"Emmy, I think it would be best if you let me drive you. You seem pretty shaken up and I don't want anything to happen to you. Please."

Emmy started to refuse, but then, seeing the worry on Greg's face as well as Westley's, she finally nodded. "Ok. Greg lock up the house please."

The drive was gut-wrenching for Emmy. She may hate her family, and she might not speak to them, but that didn't mean she wanted any of them to die. That had never crossed her mind. Ian was the brother she had always been closest to as a child. The thought of losing him with the last words they had spoken to each other that of anger made her sick to her stomach.

Westley could tell how upset Emmy was. He didn't know what was wrong, and so far she didn't seem ready to talk. He was new to her life, and he knew it was hard enough for her to have him come along for something like this. Greg too was sullen and silent in the backseat, clearly worried about Emmy just like he was.

Emmy stared out the window in the passenger seat of her truck as Westley sped toward her birthplace. As much as she hated the thought of going back there, she knew this was the one reason she could not stay away. Even if she still harbored many ill feelings toward her family for turning their backs on her, she refused to let her brother die without being there, even if it killed her.

Westley studied Emmy's profile periodically. He could see the thought of returning to her family home was taking its toll on her. He felt he needed to say something.

"Emmy, I want you to know, I understand this is a family matter, and you don't need to worry about me saying anything about what I see or hear while we are there."

Emmy glanced at Westley and smiled, muttering a quiet thank you. Westley could tell she had hardly realized she was speaking. Her soulful blue eyes were wide with fear, and Westley wasn't completely sure the fear was due to the unknown outcome of the emergency.

Behind the two, the teenage boy showed much less consideration as he rambled on with question after question.

"What happened, Emmy? Where are we going anyway?"

Emmy sighed as she glanced back at the teenage boy she cared immensely for. "My brother has been in a car accident, and we are going to the hospital in my hometown, Charlotte, North Carolina."

Greg's reply was a silent but visible O. He fiddled with his fingers a few minutes, unsure if he should engage Emmy in more conversation or not.

Instead, he said, "I didn't know you had any brothers."

Emmy nodded absently, her gaze fixed on the blurring images outside her window.

"Yes, Greg, I have three. My family is no longer included in my life, but even so, I will not allow my brother to die without seeing him one last' time. Especially Ian."

Greg frowned. "Is that why you said families are good at abandoning us when we need them most? Why even go back, if that's the case?"

"They are, at least some, but you should always try to be different. You should treat people how you want to be treated. If more people wore compassion on their sleeves the world would be a better place by far."

Greg nodded solemnly before falling silent as he, too, looked off into the distance through the window. Westley peered at Emmy and raised a brow. Interesting theory for a woman who was so good at shutting people out of her life.

"I cannot imagine it'll be easy going back, Emmy, having to face all the people you have avoided for so long. Are you sure you're ready for this?" Westley watched the emotions play across her face. It was the most open he had ever seen her.

Looking at Westley's profile as he kept his eyes on the road ahead, Emmy wasn't sure if she was grateful he was here or not.

"No, I'm not ready to go back, or to see any of them again, but I don't have much choice in the matter. They may have turned their backs on me, but I'll not do the same when my brother is asking for me on his deathbed. Just because I'm willing to come to him does not mean I've forgiven any of them."

Emmy stared out the window once more as the lights of cities and houses flashed past in a blur. When small droplets of rain began to patter down on the truck, she watched as the tiny rivulets of water ran down the glass through which she stared. She could feel all the old anger and hurt bubbling back up to the surface. She had tried to overcome her pain, and the anger she felt toward her family, but it seemed even twelve long years could not truly numb the pain of the past. It took every ounce of selfcontrol she had to keep from falling apart.

Westley, intent on keeping them safe on their drive tried his best to ignore the woman beside him and focus on the road ahead. It was proving harder and harder the closer they came to her hometown and her painful past. He could sense the battle raging within her, could see her reflection as she studied the rain outside. He could see the anguish in the plains of her face, with the tears silently streaming down her cheeks.

Again he felt the overwhelming urge to pull this woman up against him, to embrace her and protect her from the demons she seemed to harbor. He felt his fists clenching in response to her pain, and wished it were so simple. If he could chase away the haunting grief she felt, he would gladly do so, just to see her smile once more.

∞∞∞∞

-6-

Walking into the hospital in her hometown, Emmy still couldn't believe she was here, that she had come back to the place of her torment. Twelve years was a long time to avoid the past. Still, her demons plagued her, and in the back of her mind, it was all too easy to remember the night that had ruined her life, and her relationship with her family. She didn't know what would happen when she finally saw their faces for the first time.

The nurses had directed them to the surgery and ICU waiting area upon their arrival. Emmy felt as though she were in a daze. Her outer bearing was cold like stone, but on the inside, she was quaking. Westley found himself caught in the mystery and drama of Emmy's life, but it didn't feel wrong to be here with her.

Again he found himself wondering about the events that had played out to make her so terrified of the prospect of returning home and seeing her family again.

He would not ask her, but he hoped in time to learn what had happened so he might be able to help her heal. If nothing else, Westley wanted to be there for her, to offer her comfort, support, and friendship. He was determined to show her there were people in this world she could rely on.

Vadetta Everhart looked up in awe as her only daughter walked into the room. It had been so many long years since she had lain eyes on her fiery-haired daughter. She had changed so much from the tall thin young woman of sixteen that Vadetta remembered. She was a beautiful woman now, with the figure and looks women would kill for. The physical attribute that appeared to have changed the most about Emmy in the long years that had passed were her eyes.

Her blue eyes that had once been fiery and filled with life were now cold, hard, and untouchable. Standing, Vadetta took a step toward her daughter.

"Emmy, Emmy, is that you? I cannot believe you are here. You've become so beautiful."

Westley watched as Emmy's spine stiffened at the sound of her mother's voice. Turning her icy glare upon the woman, Emmy's chin rose stubbornly.

"Vadetta, you look poised as ever. Kindly tell me where Ian is so I can get this over with. I have things I need to get back to."

As she looked away from her mother, Emmy noticed her two eldest brothers walking toward her. The expression in their eyes was uncertain. Vadetta's heart sank. It was true, Emmy would never forgive them. Vadetta knew she couldn't blame her daughter. They had all made the wrong decision that night. They were all to blame for sweet Grace's death.

Emmy's gaze was far from passive as she watched her brothers come forward across the room. All of the anger and hurt she felt bubbled toward the surface. These were her older brothers, the ones who were supposed to protect her, not abandon her.

Miranda had been watching the scene unfold in worry. She decided it would be best if she interfered before things became too heated and Emmy fled. Taking Emmy's arm, she looked into the now grown face of her once close friend.

"Emmy, please come with me. I want to take you to Ian right away. He's been asking for you all night."

Allowing Miranda to pull her toward the double doors in the hallway, Emmy ground her teeth in frustration. "I should not have come."

Miranda shook her head. "No, Emmy, don't say that. You are here, you came when Ian needed you, and I cannot tell you how much that means to me, to him. Your name is the only thing he has muttered at all since waking."

The surprise that flowed through Emmy was obvious to Miranda. Pulling her through the doors and toward her husband's room, she said, "He is still in critical condition, and they are not certain he will pull through this. He broke several bones in his body, punctured a rib, and has internal bleeding. They operated once earlier, but believe he will likely need at least one more operation once he has stabilized. He's awake, but the visits need to remain short."

Nodding her head, Emmy left Miranda by the door as she entered the room labeled ICU1. Approaching the bed, she looked down at the battered and bruised man. He didn't resemble the brother she remembered, with half his face in bandages, and the other half black and blue. His body was covered in IV lines, and bandages. His left leg was covered in a cast and suspended from the ceiling. His right arm lay in a sling and split. He was a mess.

Dried blood clung to his blond hair, and Emmy felt the first waves of sympathy wash through her. As she came to stand beside him, he shifted slightly, wincing from the pain it caused.

"Is someone there?" His voice cracked. "Miranda? Is she here? Emmy. I must speak to her. Will not die until I do..."

Taking a deep breath to soothe her nerves, Emmy spoke.

"It's me, Ian. Emmy." She knew he could not see her, and for that she was grateful. She felt as though all of her composure was slipping.

A look of utter relief washed over Ian's swollen face. "Oh thank god, Emmy. I need to talk to you before I..."

"Shut up, Ian. You are not going to die. You will get through this. You have a wife and children waiting for you to come home."

Ian made the attempt to grin. "I just didn't want to die without talking to you. I wish I could see you, Emmy. I know you're beautiful from the magazine photos I've seen. Will you hear me out, please?"

When she didn't answer right away, Ian forged ahead anyway. "You don't know how badly I regret what happened to you every day of my life. I was so wrong, Emmy. I made the worst decision of my life. When Pam called and told me you were in the hospital, that they didn't know if you would make it, I waited in the waiting room the entire time. You wouldn't see me. I never told anyone this Emmy, but I saw her before she died."

Ian heard the gasp that tore from Emmy's throat. Tears filled and overflowed from her blue eyes. When she spoke, her voice was thick with them. "You saw my Grace?"

Ian started to nod, but the pain quickly stopped him. Wincing in pain, he said, "Yes. I held her in my arms, she was so tiny, and beautiful. Looking into her eyes, I saw the truth, Emmy. She made me realize you would never have run away if you'd been covering up your mistake. You told us the truth that night."

Emmy was openly sobbing by this point. She tried to keep it quiet, but she could not control the overflow of tears. When she answered him, she didn't care that her voice was thick with emotion. "Yes, Ian. I told you all the truth."

Tears had begun to flow down Ian's swollen face as he whispered, "Can you ever forgive me, Emmy?"

Taking a deep ragged breath, Emmy said, "You hurt me the most, Ian. I loved you so much. I looked up to you all my life, and when I needed you the most, you betrayed me. I am not sure anyone could forgive something like that."

Turning on her heel, Emmy fled from the room, from her brother and all the haunting memories he brought with him.

Coming into the waiting room, trying to gather her composure, Emmy found herself facing all the people in the world she wanted to run from. Groaning silently to herself, she tried to collect her wits. All of that went out the window when a moment later she heard a voice from the past that made her blood freeze.

"Why, hello darling. Emmy, it's been such a long time sweetheart. I never thought you would come back here."

Turning very slowly to face the nightmare from her past, Emmy found herself face to face with the one person she hated most in life. Her eyes lit with fury at the sight of him.

"What the hell are you doing here?" Turning to face her mother and brothers, she asked in a voice filled with disgust, "Is this supposed to be some sort of sick joke for you all? How dare you ask me to come here knowing this Bastard would be here!"

Vadetta shook her head anxiously. "No Emmy, he is not supposed to be here!" Spinning around toward the man, she narrowed her eyes. "What are you doing here Malcolm Coone? Ian made it clear he did not want you here. He has not called you his friend in a long time."

Stepping forward and laying a calming hand on his mother's shoulder, Aaron Everhart said, "I told him about the accident mama. I did not expect him to come here though."

Looking up at the man in question, Aaron sighed. "You should not have come here, Malcolm. You need to leave."

Malcolm shrugged his shoulders nonchalantly. Stepping toward Emmy, he gave her a loathsome smile. "Too bad about our daughter, eh Emmy. Sure enjoyed making her though."

With her face flushing scarlet red, Emmy stepped forward in rage. Balling her hand into a fist, she planted it straight into Malcolm's face.

"She was not your daughter. Nothing so innocent and pure could ever have come from a pig like you."

Reacting instantly, Malcolm reached toward Emmy's throat, seeming to have forgotten about the presence of her family. Westley waited in horror for someone to intercede, but when it was clear they would not, he stepped forward, wrapping his hand around Malcolm's wrist and twisting.

"Let go of her."

Malcolm groaned in pain and let go of Emmy.

Glaring at Westley, he muttered, "You'll pay for that." Cradling his hand, he sneered at Emmy before storming from the hospital.

Emmy watched him leave in a state of shock. She didn't want to evaluate what Westley had just done for her. This whole night had been too much for her. Today, she had hit her breaking point. Never again would she run from her demons. Spinning around to face her mother and brothers, Emmy glared daggers at them.

"How dare you allow that man here? I cannot believe you all! Are you all so insipid that you are still certain of his side of things? Are you all so blind?"

Stepping forward to face the wrath of his sister, Aaron said, "Come on Emmy, you were always a wild child, you swooned over him half your life. So when he got you pregnant you got scared. You lied to save your hide from mom and dad. We all know you had wanted to marry him. Is it so far to go to imagine you making an unwise choice and sleeping with him?"

Feeling the sting of his words, and the utter disbelief that her own brother could stand here and say such things after all of these years, even after Malcolm's little display, Emmy was beyond words. She glared at him.

Taking a deep breath, Emmy looked each of them square in the eye. "Is it so hard to imagine that your perfect friend, that son of a bitch was capable of raping your little sister? Did you think me so low I would actually give myself up to him? Why would I cover up my pregnancy with a lie if I had wanted to marry him so badly? Had I come to you all sooner, when the bruises all over me were still fresh, maybe then you might have seen through his lies?"

Vadetta stared in horror at her daughter. For many years she had wondered about the truth of what had happened with her daughter and Malcolm. Standing there now, she knew the answer. She could see it in her daughter's eyes.

Emmy stepped backward away from the three of them. "You want to know the truth of what happened that night? I will tell you. We went to the races like always. Unlike always, however, I found myself alone with Malcolm as Aaron and Connor ran off with their dates, and Ian and Miranda disappeared. Malcolm offered me a ride home, so I accepted. He had been our friend since we were kids.

Before he gave me a ride home, he led me under the bleachers, saying he wanted to talk about something. Everyone had left. It was just the two of us there. Malcolm came onto me. I will not lie. At first, I was happy, thinking that maybe he felt the same crush I felt for him. Then, he tried to pull my dress up. I told him to stop, and he pinned me down. I struggled, telling him over and over to stop. Begging him to stop. He started hitting me. He said he'd slit my throat if I moved.

Every time I tried to pull away, he hit me harder. Then, he raped me. He took my virginity, something that was not his to take. I cried, screamed, but no one came. He told me he had been waiting a long time to get me alone."

Shaking both in anger and in fear as the memories of that night washed over her, Emmy glared at her family as tears fell unbidden from her eyes. "I told Ian. He was the one I thought I could trust. I needed his help, but he told you, Mama. You and dad, you turned on me. I ran that night, not because I had lied, but because I was terrified you would make me marry that vile man and he would be able to do that to me again and again for the rest of my life!

I ran on foot, getting as far away as I could. By the time I felt I was far enough away, I got sick. My baby was born three months early, she never even had a chance. You all knew I was there at the hospital, dying. Ian was the only one who bothered to show up. You all let me lose my baby. I didn't want her at first, knowing how I came to be pregnant, but then, I started to love her. Do any of you know what it feels like to have a man force you to have sex? To violate that most sacred part of you? No! You don't! I loved that delicate little girl the entire two days she got to live. Why couldn't any of you love me even half that much?"

Vadetta's eyes had filled with tears at her daughter's words. She had never known the details of what had happened before. She never knew her pregnant daughter had walked the entire way to another state. She never knew about the sickness that caused her to go into labor prematurely. Why had she ever doubted her daughter?

How had she been so blind, so foolish? She realized the truth of her daughter's words. She and her husband would have tried to make her marry Malcolm to keep their name out of the gutter. Walking forward, Vadetta tried to embrace her daughter, but Emmy pulled away from her and fled through the hospital doors.

Pamela and David arrived not long after the confrontation with Emmy and her family. Staring in anger at Connor, Aaron, and Vadetta, Pam shook her head.

"Don't you think you have put that woman through enough? She was a sixteen-year-old child, alone, and pregnant!"

Looking into Aaron's blank face, she asked him, "How do you like your comfortable little life, Aaron? You have a wife, kids. Don't you think Emmy deserved to be happy? To have all of those things? She never married, and likely never will."

Looking into the faces of the three Everhart's, she continued in anger. "You know what else, Emmy is so afraid of men after what happened she has never even allowed another to touch her. The only time she has known what it was to be physical with a man was when that pig raped her."

Vadetta's tears welled from her eyes. Wringing her hands, she cried, "I never meant to hurt her, I never meant to run her off..."

Pam glared at Vadetta. "You. She needed you the most. Do you realize she almost died while trying to keep her baby alive? How was she supposed to know she had a rare form of anemia when she had no one to care for her? Do you know it was your name she called out while giving birth? Again and again, she cried for her mama. You should have seen the tormented faces of the hospital staff, listening to her, watching her struggle to live, and knowing her baby probably wouldn't make it. None of you deserve her!"

Westley approached Emmy slowly where she sat crumpled on the curb outside. His questions had been answered tonight, and in many ways, he wished they hadn't. He had never imagined the truth would be so terrible. Never imagined the reason for the brokenness in her eyes could be such an awful event. It was no wonder she hated her family. No surprise she refused to allow men into her life.

Westley realized what an amazing woman she truly was, to have lived through such torture, and still have the compassion to raise a teenage boy with love and kindness. Lowering himself to sit beside Emmy, but careful not to touch her, Westley wasn't sure exactly what to say.

Emmy lifted her swollen puffy, and yet still so beautiful eyes to him. In a cracking voice, she asked, "Why did you help me, Westley?"

Westley was taken aback by the question. "What do you mean why? I wasn't about to stand by and watch some guy choke you."

Emmy shrugged. "No one else cared. You are the only one who tried to help me, and you're a virtual stranger to me."

Westley watched the emotions running rampant in her dark blue eyes. "I would help you any day, Emmy. And you don't feel like a stranger to me."

Emmy attempted a smile, but it was halfhearted. "Well, I guess you know more about me than you'd like to know. Sure you want a boss that's as messed up as me?"

Grinning, Westley touched his fingers gently to Emmy's tear-streaked cheek. "No. But I wouldn't mind having a friend who's a little messed up."

Emmy pulled away, as Westley had expected her to. Removing her gaze from him, she looked off into the distance. "Why? Why would you want to tangle yourself up in my mess?"

Westley shrugged. "Some people are worth wading through the mess to find, Emmy. We all have baggage, some just more than others. The person you are now is the person I am interested in. If I have to chase a few demons away to be your friend, then so be it."

For the first time since her childhood, Emmy felt the awakening of feelings for a man. She didn't know why he was here, why he had come back from Ireland, or to her farm, but she admitted she was grateful for his presence in her life. She didn't trust him completely, but after what he had done that night, she thought perhaps she should get to know this man a little better. Perhaps he was worth it.

Westley knew it would be a long drive home, and he offered to check them into a hotel instead, but Emmy insisted she was done here. She wanted nothing to do with this place, and she had done what she came to do. She had spoken to Ian, and she did not think he was going to die. Westley didn't want to push her too much, so he sucked down a gallon of coffee, and drove the long road home.

Along the drive, during which Emmy and Greg slept most of the way, Westley found himself revisiting the events of the night. He could not believe Emmy had been the victim of a brutal rape, and he felt his anger rise up again at the thought of any man laying their hands on her in such a way. He felt again the surge of protectiveness over this woman that he hardly knew.

Thinking back over the numerous magazine clippings he had collected about her when initially asked to write an article about her, Westley did some quick math in his head. If he had his calculations right, Emmy had risen to the top of her equestrian class within only a few short years of facing all of this. He knew she had begun showing for trainers before her eighteenth birthday, and that at eighteen she had placed amongst the top three riders in her division. Shaking his head, Westley again thought she was something else.

To have had to face such horrors in her youth, and yet still hold the grim determination and love of horses to see her dreams through was an amazing trait in itself. Westley knew not many teenagers would have that kind of fortitude. She did it all on her own too. Showing up at a barn after losing her baby, and nearly her life must have taken all the willpower she had left. Everything he learned about this woman only made him want to know more.

Arriving at the farm on the cusp of daybreak, just as the sun was rising over the hills to the east, Westley glanced at Emmy to find her watching him. Slightly startled to find her awake, he gave her a small smile.

"Morning. You know Emmy, after the night you've had why don't you go ahead and head inside, and I'll take care of things out here."

Greg laughed from the backseat. Muttering good luck beneath his breath. Westley sent the boy a mocking wink before glancing back at Emmy. To his consternation, the woman had already hopped out of the truck and headed toward the barn. Cursing beneath his breath and ignoring the laughing teenager, he ran up behind her.

"Emmy, really it's ok." Before he could say anymore, Emmy held up a hand to silence him.

"Westley, you did more for me in the last twenty-four hours than my entire family has done in over a decade. You drove to another state and back, and I know you must be exhausted. Taking care of this farm is something I have been doing on my own for the past three years. So, go into the house, Greg can show you to your room, and get some sleep."

Westley chewed his lip as Emmy turned her back on him and strode stiffly away. Behind him, Greg cleared his throat.

"Sorry Mr. Galway, but she's a fight you are never gonna win. She works the hardest when she's upset about something. Likely she won't come back in till after sunset.

She has her routine, and unless you want her to rethink the job, you'd best just follow me."

Westley couldn't help himself. He chuckled. Nodding, he shrugged his shoulders. "All right, kid. You probably know her better than I do."

Emmy poured her heart into chores that morning. With the ever-faithful Rainy at her side, she plowed through feeding and stall cleaning without sparing a thought for anything. Stopping after chores had been done to see the gray colt, Emmy allowed herself a moment's reprieve. Leaning her back against the post just inside the pasture the colt was sharing with Fiorghr'a, she let out a deep sigh.

She was bone tired, emotionally drained, and just plain done caring right now. She kept her eyes on the colt as Fio made her way toward Emmy curiously. The mare leaned her big head down, nuzzling and sniffing at Emmy. Behind her, Emmy could see the gray colt throw his tantrum. He pawed, bucked, reared, and tossed his head with vigor. He was truly annoyed that this human had taken the affection of his herd.

Emmy chuckled. The colt pinned his ears and snorted. Sighing, Emmy speculated about the colt's future. Would she ever be able to tame him, or would he be a beautiful lawn ornament? She hoped with all her soul he would come around. The way he had looked sailing over those jumps had been something out of a fairy tale. He was exactly what she needed, now she just needed to figure out a way to let him know she was what he needed as well.

Hearing the sound of car tires on gravel, Emmy hefted herself up to walk back to the barn. Glancing at her watch, she frowned. She had forgotten Michelle was going to be here at seven to start her new job. Emmy shrugged. There were plenty of other things she could teach her besides feeding and stall cleaning.

Michelle, clearly excited to start her day with all the youthful exuberance of a child, jogged over to Emmy. She began rattling on about how excited she was to be there. Any other day Emmy would have been happy for the upbeat teen, but today it grated on her nerves. Smiling at Michelle, she attempted to reel her in.

"I'm glad your excited Michelle. I have already taken care of morning chores, so if you're up for it we can work some horses before today's lessons start."

Michelle smiled widely. "Oh, that would be great. I cannot wait to get up into a saddle again."

Nodding, Emmy, handed her a paper. "That is a list of things that can be done if you finish up early. It also has the name of a few horses I would like you to exercise on a daily basis. I picked them out to match your skill level as best as possible. Some you may find a smidge boring, while others a slight challenge. Go ahead and pull one out and I'll grab mine."

Twenty minutes later, Michelle trotted easily around the outdoor arena on Scotch on Rocks, a frisky dark chestnut filly Emmy was training for her contract with Mr. Geraldo. The young woman looked good on the six-year-old, and the filly was responding well to her cues. The big bullheaded colt beneath Emmy was another story entirely.

Sighing in exasperation at the colts antics to evade the reins, Emmy gently but firmly corrected him. Once she had him walking a relatively straight line toward the other end of the arena, she asked him to reverse arc and worked him gently through the cues. Smiling, Emmy ran her hand down the colt's neck.

"There you go, Shamrock. Stop fighting and the pressure will go away. You'll get it soon enough big guy."

The colt felt wound up like he hadn't been out enough, and Emmy made a mental note to have him turned out on his days off. Apparently, he was one of those horses that didn't do so well stalled up. Altogether, the ride wasn't too bad, a couple flighty attempts here and there, and one small crow hop in refusal. Easy enough to remedy.

For the next few hours, she and Michelle rode in harmony, each with their own list of horses to ride. She had to admit, she was definitely happy with what she had seen from the young woman so far. She had a good seat, soft quiet hands, a calm demeanor, and clearly had received a good amount of training somewhere. Emmy knew this young woman would be an asset to their little farm. She looked forward to having Michelle show some of the more intermediate level horses and had the feeling the young woman would progress well into advanced riding in no time.

As they exercised their horses, Emmy threw a comment or two her way, suggesting better use of her legs, a slightly different cue. In essence, she was giving the girl a tune-up. Michelle was gracious and over the moon to receive any instruction at all from such an accomplished rider like Emmy.

Westley watched the two riding from the porch. He liked that about this house, the ability to see the barns and both arenas from the house. He noticed Emmy working hard with one of the horses, a strong headed dark gray horse who liked to chomp the bit a lot. By the end of their ride, however, the colt had collected into a smooth ride, and begun responding to her cues much more easily. Westley smiled to himself.

The woman rode with the feather light movements of a very accomplished equestrian. He liked that about Emmy. She rarely used her crop, and she seemed to have endless patience with both her horses and the people around her. Thinking about her soft hands brought unwanted images to Westley's mind. After what he had learned about Emmy's past last night, he realized he had no right to have any sexual thoughts about this woman at all.

He knew he would have to tread much more carefully with her from now on. She needed a man who knew how to control himself, who knew how to be a real man and treat a woman right. Westley was determined to show Emmy that not all men in this world were the scum her first encounter had been.

Feeling something cold and wet touch his hand, Westley nearly leaped from his seat. Looking down, he exhaled when he realized it was just the young collie he had seen romping around the farm. Laughing, he stroked the fluffy red head of the wiggling puppy. With her long thin face and big bright eyes, she was quite the character.

"And just who might you be? You're awful cute, but you sure scared the hell outta me, pup."

Behind him, Greg came through the screen door. "That's Feather. She's pretty young still. She gets in trouble for chasing the hens a lot, so I try to keep her around the house. Emmy adopted her from a rescue to keep Rainy company. You ask me, the only one Rainy ever notices is Emmy."

Westley glanced in the direction Greg indicated with a nod of his head. Sure enough, the big mostly black long-haired shepherd sat at attention outside the arena, eyes focused solely on Emmy. Westley smiled. He had noticed the way the dog stuck to the woman's hip with an intense adoration.

Greg cleared his throat. "I'm going to head out there, lessons are going to start soon. Wednesdays are usually one of the busiest for students."

Glancing at Westley, Greg held eye contact for a moment before continuing, "What happened to Emmy was terrible huh?"

When Westley nodded, Greg swallowed. "I wish it hadn't. She's a really good person, even if she makes me help at those gross breeding's. I wanted to say thanks, for standing up for her last night, but if you hurt her in any way, I'll shoot you myself."

Westley tried to keep his smile at bay as he watched Greg walk off. The kid clearly had a lot of compassion for Emmy, and Westley was again curious how she ended up with the kid. Standing and stretching, he whistled to the pup and headed after Greg toward the barn where Emmy and the new young woman were putting away their tack.

Emmy was immediately aware of the moment when Westley's attractive form entered the barn. It irritated the hell out of her the way her body seemed to be hyperaware of him, even from a distance. Gritting her teeth, she tried to focus her unruly thoughts on her task at hand. On the one hand, she was grateful he was here, and on the other, she was beginning to regret the decision to hire him based on the distraction he had become.

Emmy put her horse away and leaned against the doorway of the barn. Sipping her water, she studied the nearly black horse romping around in the pasture with Fio. She needed to figure out a way to gain his trust.

"Greg, from now on, I think we will forfeit graining Fio and the colt. There is plenty of grass there to sustain them, and I want to use grain as a tool for that colt. In a few months, I'm going to have to separate him from Fio when I send her for breeding, and I need to have gained some kind of communication with him before that."

Greg nodded and walked toward the board to change the feeding schedule for the two. Westley stepped up beside Emmy. Looking in the direction she was, he asked, "What's wrong with the horse that you cannot just catch him?"

Emmy smiled. Her eyes seemed unfocused, as though she was not even aware he was there. "He's...special."

Westley glanced from her to the pasture several times. When it became clear she would divulge nothing more, he shrugged.

"Emmy, I spoke to the man where I have been boarding my herd, and he can deliver them tomorrow if that works out all right for you? The only two that really need stalls are the two stallions."

Emmy's eyes refocused as she rotated to face Westley. "Yeah, that sounds fine. I have a few lessons this afternoon, would you like to take today to go gather your stuff and get settled in? We can handle everything here, and you can start officially in the morning."

Cocking his head to the side and lifting an eyebrow in amusement, Westley lowered his voice as he asked, "Emmy, are you trying to get rid of me already?"

Looking into those green eyes that made her feel all too exposed, Emmy laughed nervously. Yes, she was.

"Of course not, Westley, I just thought you could use the time to get situated that's all."

Westley could see through her act, but after learning of her dark past last night, he was not going to push her.

Instead, he sent her a devilishly charming grin, shrugged his shoulders, and turned away, saying over his shoulder, "Sounds good. See you tonight, Emmy."

Why was it that those four very simple and innocent words, when spoken in his deep lilting Irish accent sent shivers down her entire body? Emmy was unequivocally grateful the man's back was turned so he didn't see her struggling to reel in all the sensual thoughts that came to her mind. She wanted to kick herself. What the hell was wrong with her? She felt ridiculous like she was a filly in heat for the first time. Shaking her head, she ground her teeth. No. she would not allow this attraction she felt toward him to distract her.

That afternoon's lessons were trying to say the least. The blond was half an hour late, causing Emmy to have no choice but to run two lessons into each other. After the blond and her daughter had gone, failing to care for their horse, again, Emmy wanted to scream. Keeping her face passive, she continued watching her two students, determined not to show her frustration in front of them.

Their mother, a delicate brunette with unending patience and the sweetest personality she had ever encountered approached the fence once the others were gone.

"Goodness, Emmy, I do not know how you put up with that woman! She is always late, she never takes care of their horse, and she sits here primping the entire time!"

Emmy glanced at Eleanor Sommer's. Smiling, she shrugged. "Not all the parents are as great as you, Eleanor. I just have to deal with it, at least until I have enough students to pick and choose."

Eleanor looked offended. "Emmy! You are Emmy Everhart! Of course, you can pick and choose. There is a reason I pulled the girls from their trainer and came here as soon as I heard you were accepting students. You are above and beyond, and you should have the right to choose who is worth your time."

Emmy blushed. "Eleanor, that's really sweet of you to say, but until I have paid the Ryans back for all their contributions to this place, I need the profit. Besides, the daughter isn't as bad as the mom."

Glancing at the two girls riding in the arena, Emmy smiled. "I wanted to talk to you about your girls. There is a show coming up in a couple weeks, and I think it would be a great confidence builder if Sarah rode Bell in a couple classes."

Eleanor nodded enthusiastically. "That would be great Emmy. What about Jen? I have been talking to Fred about looking for another horse. Old Sebastian is too old I think for competitions, and you know she wants to jump."

Emmy considered that for a moment. "You know, Sebastian is a great schooling horse, he's gentle, well-mannered, and I could use another beginner horse here. I would be willing to make a partial trade if you guys were interested. I have a few prospective horses that might be at Jen's level."

Eleanor's face lit up. "Oh, Emmy, that would be amazing. If Jen knew old Sebastian was here with you it would be so much easier for her. She's so attached to the old chestnut."

"Why don't you guys come back tomorrow, or sometime this week, and we can have her ride the horses I have in mind, to see if she clicks with any of them."

By the time Emmy wound down the night's chores, she was exhausted. She realized she hadn't eaten anything, and her emotions were wearing thin. She knew if anything else happened she would probably lose it. She had just decided to head in and call it a night as she walked past the pastures when she glanced toward Fio and the gray colt. Stopping, she studied the scene with curiosity.

Fio was off in the distance, happily munching away on the bluegrass that grew in lush amounts here. The colt, however, was not at her side as was his usual habit. Tonight, he stood near the gate, ears twitching as he seemed to wait for something. Emmy, allowing her curiosity to get the better of her, walked over to the fence and leaned against the gate.

"What's up big fellow? You waiting for your grain? Why aren't you with your lady friend?"

In a manner that was not completely usual to him, the colt stepped tentatively forward. Frowning, Emmy studied him. This was unusual. The colt had never shown even the slightest interest in her before. Stepping into the pasture, Emmy hopped up onto the top railing to watch him, eliciting an annoyed snort from the horse.

Looking over him, Emmy admired all the grace and beauty in the clean smooth lines of the horse. His black coat gleamed, and the patches of graying dapples showing through at his shoulders and flanks added a mysteriousness to him. There was a new patch, a small streak of dark gray running about an inch or two down the left side of his face. Emmy smiled at it. She rifled through her memories, trying to remember if Geraldo had ever mentioned the colt's name, but she came up blank.

As she sat there, studying the impressive looking colt, Emmy allowed the events of the previous day to finally catch up to her. Bowing her head, she felt the sobs rack her body as she allowed herself to release the emotions she had pushed to the side all day. Hot wet tears ran down her face, and she didn't care. She needed to deal with what had happened. Seeing that man again had broken a part of her she thought had been healed.

She thought she had put it all in the past, she thought she had moved on, but seeing his face, hearing his words, it had felt like the whole thing was happening again. She had been so afraid, despite her brave words, deep down there had been so much fear. In her mind, she could still see it playing out, every touch, every blow, and every painful part of that horrid night.

Lifting her head to gaze up at the setting sun, she wished it would soothe her, the beauty of it, the serenity of it all, but she felt it was all for naught. Nothing would ever truly dull the pain she felt. A few yards away from her, the colt's ears twitched several times. He tossed his head, snorted and pawed, unsure what this powerful emotion was that this woman felt. He could sense her feelings, but it was unfamiliar to him this human emotion.

Over an hour passed as Emmy sat there, allowing her grief to fuel her tears. Surprisingly, the colt stayed there, watching her. Occasionally, he would take a tentative step forward, curious about this human. Emmy was aware of the horse, but at that moment, she didn't have it in her to acknowledge what his actions could mean. She had sensed the horse was not truly mean-spirited, just fearful.

Closing her eyes, Emmy tried her best to clear her mind. She tried meditation, to allow all of it to wash from her mind, but instead, another image filled the space.

Westley. Groaning, Emmy shook her head in frustration. That was not what she wanted to see. Why was her mind torturing her with images of the handsome Irishman when she needed emptiness? Something touched her knee. Emmy's eyes snapped open with full awareness.

The colt had moved much closer to her and had stretched his muzzle forward, keeping himself as far as possible away from her, but still wanting to fill his inquisitiveness. Emmy wanted to laugh at the comical way the horse stood, so afraid to fully approach her, and yet so stretched out. Instead, she remained very still, and unmoving. The colts muzzle wiggled against her knee, and slowly, Emmy brought her hand forward with a sugar cube.

Smelling the sweetness of the treat, the colt moved his muzzle ever closer. When his sensitive lips brushed her hand, he jerked back, squealing in alarm. Emmy smiled. Within moments, he came back for more. When he left his muzzle in her hand for an extended period, Emmy tickled his chin with her fingers, to which the colt's reply was stomping his leg. Emmy did laugh then.

The sound sent the colt rocketing off kicking and stomping as though attacking an invisible threat. The southern breeze chose that moment to pick up, billowing gently through the willows around her, and pulling her hair loose from her braid. Smiling, Emmy nodded.

"Yes, that's what you are. Wild, and free, finicky like the southern breeze. But not a breeze, no you're more like the wind. The strong, fierce southern wind.

-7-

Westley lay awake late into the night, his mind filled with images of Emmy. Why it was this woman stirred his blood like no other, he still could not say. There was just some strong connection, both physical and emotional between them, and despite both of their efforts to ignore it, it remained. In fact, it didn't just remain, it grew, developing branches with each day they spent around each other.

In the short month, he had been here, Westley had struggled to keep his feelings under control. There were times he had to leave her presence altogether, just to keep from acting upon the urge to touch her, kiss her. Groaning, Westley stood. Pulling on his jeans, he headed outside. He needed the rush of the cold southern wind in his face, to cool the flames of desire he felt burning for the most unobtainable woman he had ever met.

Striding across the lawn, he headed for the small personal barn where Emmy kept the stallions. Inside, he didn't bother to turn on the light. He knew the stall he sought. He knew the color, the facial distinctions, knew, even the rough whinny of this horse. He had watched this deep red chestnut colt as it left its mother the night of its birth. He had watched him grow from a strong promising colt, into the big, fearsome bloody colored stallion he was now.

He had nurtured him, bathed him, fed him, and trained him. He had been the most promising horse at Galway stables. He had been Westley's dream, the culmination of his breeding endeavors. He had chosen the dam and sire for this horse himself. He had slaved over breeding books, and progeny reports. He had researched the careers of each bloodline until he could recite them by heart. And then, he had watched this horse kill his beloved brother.

Stopping in front of the stall, just out of reach of the horse, who tried in vain to reach the man, to nuzzle him, to sniff him, to gain the attention of the one he had known the best. To him, this was his rider, his partner, his most trusted friend. But that friend had been gone a long time. He had left him. They had both left him. The stallion tossed his head, whinnying in frustration that he couldn't touch the hand of the man who had bonded with him before any other.

Westley studied the large soulful eyes of the Irish Warmblood stallion. He felt anger, hatred, and pain when he looked at this magnificent animal. He saw his brother, Joseph, so full of life. He saw him lying crumpled on the greens of the cross-country course. Dead.

Glaring at the horse in anger, Westley took a step away. "You were supposed to protect him. You were supposed to keep him alive! I gave you everything I had, every hour of my life, every ounce of love, and training I knew how. And you killed him. Why? Why didn't you take that jump like you had been trained?"

Westley fell to his knees, hiding his face in his palms, he wept. He wept for the wasted life of his young brother, he wept for the horse he had once loved above everything in his life. He should have sold the horse a long time ago.

Emmy watched Westley from the porch. Even from here, she could see the distance he kept from this one horse. Emmy had noticed it the first day they came. He doted on his horses, cared deeply for each one, except this one. This horse he refused to touch. When he looked at the stallion, Emmy had seen anger flare in his eyes. She could not begin to imagine what would cause such a reaction in this compassionate man.

When the silhouette of Westley fell to his knees before the horse, Emmy felt her heart break for him. She knew he was crying, this big, powerful man. Seeing him kneel there before the horse he appeared to hate, Emmy felt tears sting her own eyes. Taking a step toward the stairs, intent on going to him, Emmy thought better of it. Perhaps he would turn her away. She realized that although the urge to comfort him was strong, she had no right, no place in this man's business.

They had both been keeping a very professional relationship during the past month, both eager to avoid the other, and she knew that to approach him now would breach that invisible hurdle that existed between them. She knew she was not ready to do any such thing, no matter how much her heart ached for this man.

Rising early the following morning, Emmy felt her spirits soar. In just a few days she would enter the first competition she had entered in nearly a year. She would be taking some of her students with her and showing some of the horses she had started herself. This was a big day for Lost Acres, and if they placed well, it would give her training stables a boost in reputation.

At the breakfast nook, Greg and Westley were already chowing into cereal like three-year-olds. Emmy sent them suspicious looks.

"What are the two of you doing up so early?"

Westley sent Greg an exaggerated wink before grinning at her.

"We got tired of you trying to show us up all the time. The horses have already been fed, and stalls mucked. So relax."

Emmy's step faltered. She glanced in shock from one to the other of them.

"Goodness. Whatever will I do with my life if you've all done my job?"

Westley chuckled at her attempt to faint. He liked this side of Emmy, the carefree happy side. "Well, you could take a ride with me today, instead of taking off by yourself."

This time, the surprise on Emmy's face was not faked. "Uh…well, actually, my garden needs weeding, perhaps today would be a good day…"

Westley didn't let her finish. "Emmy you are coming riding with me. I won't bite, I promise. Don't be such a scaredy cat."

Greg chuckled. Seeing the glare Emmy sent him, he choked on his cereal. Clearing his throat, he said, "I'm pretty sure I have homework to do… see you later."

Emmy continued to glare at him as he fled the crime scene. Turning her annoyed glare on Westley, she planted her hands on her hips.

"Why are you being so pushy about this?"

Westley gulped a deep fortifying breath as he told his eyes not to follow her hands. He had seen enough of those hips in his thoughts to last him a lifetime of torture.

"I am being pushy, Emmy, because I feel like you have been avoiding me since the night with your family. Also because you always ride out alone, and I would like to join you."

Emmy studied his darkly handsome looks. Today, he wore a black long sleeved button up. He had the arms rolled up to his elbows, exposing his thick forearms.

Emmy sighed. Oh, those forearms. The man was beyond attractive, and because this was the first man she had felt this way toward since she was a girl, she didn't quite know how to act around him. So yes, she had been avoiding him.

Emmy poured some cereal. Sitting down, she glanced up to meet his gaze and froze. The expression on his face was…knowing. She had the distinct feeling he had been aware of her perusal of his features, and she suddenly wanted to run and hide. Instead, she dug into her cereal with gusto.

Across the table, Westley bit back his laughter. God. The way she had been looking at him had just about broken his control. He made a mental note to expose his forearms more often, as apparently, Emmy had a certain interest in them. Taking another bite of his cereal, he was all too aware of the thick sexual tension in the room. How was he supposed to woo a woman who wouldn't trust him, and likely didn't even understand her own feelings? Westley felt doomed.

Outside, the pair walked toward the barns. After kissing her beloved Viewfinder on his nose, Emmy walked the aisle. She stopped in front of the big deep red chestnut. He was one of the finest looking horses she had ever seen. The horse was perfection at its finest. He was large, powerful, and exquisite. Reading the name written on the whiteboard near the stall, Emmy glanced at Westley. He was working hard to ignore the fact that she was looking at this particular horse.

"His name, Fuil Fiabhras, geez, I can barely say it. What does it mean, Westley?" Emmy waited for him to turn toward her, but he didn't.

"It's ok, it's not an easy one to say. Fuil Fiabhras. It means Bloodfever. I chose it because he was that deep red even at the moment he was foaled."

Emmy shivered at the way his Irish brogue came out. She noticed the way the stallion's ears flicked forward when Westley had said his name. The stallion's full attention was on the man behind her. Even when she stepped forward and ran her hand down the side of his satiny red face, still it was the man that kept his interest.

Emmy felt again the pull on her heartstrings. "Bloofever. I like it. It suits him. It's dark, and sensual, like him."

Turning, Emmy was about to say something else when she found Westley staring at her in the most carnal way she had ever seen. She faltered on her words. Stuttering.

"He...uh...ummm that is, he seems very bonded to you, Westley, the way he gives you his undivided attention even at just the sound of your voice."

Westley looked from her to the horse and then turned away. "I think I'll take Dorchadas out today. He looks like he needs to stretch his legs."

Emmy studied the black horse. He too was an immensely impressive animal.

"Foeger Dorchadas. What does his name mean? It sounds mysterious."

Westley chuckled. He liked Emmy's fascination with the Irish names. "It means Beautiful Darkness. He is half-brother to the red one."

Surprised, and excited, Emmy smiled as she looked at the bloody colored stallion she touched.

"Really? That is exciting. They obviously have awesome breeding. The red one, though really?"

Westley glanced at her. He tried to hide his annoyance that she was still there, doting on the one horse he couldn't stand. Shrugging, he turned back to his horse, until the words she spoke next made his blood curdle.

"You know, Westley, I think I'll take this one out. He looks like he'd be an adventure to ride."

Westley could not stop his reaction. Whirling around red-faced, he spoke louder than he meant. "No! No one rides that horse. No one!"

The stallion pulled back at the tone of Westley's voice, and Emmy took a step back as well. The anger she heard in his voice was not the Westley she had seen so far. Clearly, there was something seriously wrong here. At the moment, however, Emmy felt her defenses go up at the way in which he had spoken to her. The old fear crept to the surface, and she reacted with instinct. Turning, she fled the barn, trying to keep her own demons hidden.

Westley stood still, staring at Emmy's retreating form for several moments. Letting out a frustrated growl, he sprinted after her. He hadn't meant to raise his voice at her, hadn't meant to let that anger find its way to her, but that horse hit a nerve. Running after her, he cursed. The woman was a lot faster than he gave her credit for. Coming out of the barn, he glanced around and sighed in defeat when there was no sign of the woman.

Throwing up his hands, Westley looked all over the stables for her. When he couldn't find her there, he ransacked the house. There was no sign of her. All day, Westley roamed the farm like a madman looking for her. He was losing his mind. She was nowhere to be found, even Greg was beginning to worry.

"What the heck happened? This isn't like her at all, to take off, especially on foot. She's got to be here somewhere. Rainy is gone too, so obviously they have to be on the property. I'm sure she will come back."

Westley ran his hands through his longer than normal hair. He was worried sick, afraid he had messed up the one chance he'd had. Looking at the accusation in Greg's eyes, he blew out a long breath.

"Damn it. I messed up Greg. I lost my temper, I spoke in anger, and I wouldn't have if she would have just let it alone about that bloody horse. Why did she have to ask to ride that damn devil horse?"

Greg studied Westley's profile before he responded. He felt that Westley was a good person, and he didn't see the potential that Westley would harm Emmy, but obviously, he had upset her. Coming to sit beside him on the porch steps, he frowned down at his hands.

"Westley, what horse? Why would you get angry about her riding a horse? That doesn't really seem like you."

Westley glanced at Greg in shame. "Yeah, I know, and normally it's not. It's just that horse, the red one, there are things she doesn't understand, he... I... damn it. I just don't want anyone else to get hurt."

Riding out into the open pastures of the farm, Westley kept the deep black horse at a soft trot. He looked all over, hoping for some sign of Emmy. It would be dark soon, and she still had not come back. He was worried sick for her. He was angry at himself. He was devastated he had run her off.

Emmy had run to hide the emotions she felt overwhelming her. She realized the farther into the pasture she ran that it was an extremely immature thing to do, but she didn't care. As much as she hated to admit it, she had feelings for Westley, and they did not stop with attraction. She liked him more than any man she had known. She loved the way he was with horses, loved the way he was around people, but what he had demonstrated tonight had shown her a side of him she'd not seen before. A side of him that brought out the fear in her.

Finding the large ancient willow she had discovered on a ride, she crawled beneath its long swaying branches. Pulling her knees up to her chest, she watched the moss-covered wispy branches of the willow sway in the breeze. Resting her chin on her up-drawn knees, she allowed herself to think about Westley, to consider everything she knew about him so far, and piece it all together. The way he acted around that horse didn't fit the bill. The way he had spoken today at her mention of riding the horse did not fit. She recalled his words from long ago as they sat in a pub in Ireland.

"Once, I loved Ireland, loved it with everything in my soul, but over the last decade, I've lost so much here, faced so much grievance. I feel like there is always death awaiting me here. It's soured me to my own country."

Emmy went over and over those words in her mind. She didn't know what had happened, but she had the feeling that something terrible had happened, and it had involved the red horse. Emmy's heart broke just thinking about it. The horse obviously cared deeply for the man, and Westley must still care for the animal or he'd have gotten rid of it long ago. Whatever had happened, it had been bad enough to drive a wedge between himself and his love for the horse.

Rain pelted down into Westley's face, making him curse. It was near to dark, and the wind had picked up. He had hoped the clouds would hold, but clearly, Nature had other plans. The horse's stride was confident beneath him, and Westley found himself reminded of another horse, at another time.

The red colt had been confident and surefooted too. He had exuded prowess over the jumps. He had been one of the most graceful creatures Westley had even been privileged to ride. His dad had been pushing him to show the colt, but Westley held back. He hadn't felt the young horse was ready yet.

Shaking his head, Westley grit his teeth as he tried to dispel the memory. He would not revisit the past today, not now. He needed to find Emmy, he needed to fix things with her. Darkness was gathering around him as he rode the dark horse through the fields. Glancing around, trying to see through the rain, he almost missed the sight of the dog as it came toward him. The dog whined. Westley recognized it as Emmy's straight away.

"Where is she, girl, where's Emmy?"

Hopping off the horse, Westley watched as the dog walked to the old willow, disappearing beneath its branches. Sucking in a breath, Westley rushed after the dog. When he ducked beneath the branches, he found Emmy curled in a ball, sound asleep. Westley sighed heavily. He had never felt such relief in all his life. Scooping Emmy into his arms, he sighed at the bliss of being able to hold her.

Lifting her up onto the horse, he felt her rouse. Mumbling about gray horses, she seemed incoherent. Westley hopped into the saddle behind her. With both arms firmly behind her, he whistled for the dog and nudged the stallion back toward the farm. The stress that had left him at finding her safe only confirmed to him how deeply he really felt for this woman. Riding back to the stables with her body pressed into his, however, was misery.

Emmy fully roused as they reached the barn. She felt disgruntled, disoriented, and was acutely aware of something poking her. Wiggling, she tried to figure out what was causing the discomfort when she heard Westley growl.

"Woman, you'll have to be stopping that, or I'll no be able to control the way my body feels about you."

Emmy's entire body stiffened. Reality came flooding back to her like a full-blown tornado. When comprehension of what she was feeling hit her, she became overwrought with fear. Trying to scoot as far away from him as possible on the horse, she nearly fell off. Westley hopped down off the horse. Looking up into her wide blue eyes, he took her hand.

"Emmy, I am sorry. I'm sorry for earlier, for losing my temper, for raising my voice. I'm sorry for right now, that the attraction I feel for you has gotten the best of me, and I've scared you even more. I swear to you, you've nothing to fear from me. I would never harm not one hair on your head. Please, understand that the horse is not something I am ready to discuss and forgive me."

Emmy stared into Westley's green eyes for a long time. She could see the hurt, the regret. She could tell from the way he spoke to her, and the way he looked at her that he was sincere.

"I forgive you Westley, but if you ever speak to me in that tone again, you're out of my life for good."

Westley released the breath he hadn't realized he'd been holding. He sighed, pulling Emmy's hand with more force, he used the chance he had. Pulling her off the horse and into his arms, even just for one more brief moment, Westley inhaled the scent of her. When he released her, he stepped away and led his horse to the barn, leaving Emmy to her own thoughts.

Above him, the announcer's voice boomed across the speakers.

"Riding onto the course next is our very own Emmy Everhart. It's been a while since we've seen her, and I know we are all looking forward to watching her today. Riding the Dutch Warmblood Olympic Thunder. Good luck, Miss. Everhart."

Westley and Greg smiled at one another. It was easy to tell she was a favorite of many. Watching Emmy as she entered the arena on the nearly white horse, Westley grinned to himself. She really was something to behold. Her body flowed with the horse like poetry. Westley watched in fascination as Emmy cleared the first hurdle. Westley shook his head. His body felt every stride with her, every lift and landing as though he were there beside her. Her horse was responding well to Emmy's cues, and he seemed fearless at the jumps.

The colt didn't hesitate, not even once during the entire round. Their one penalty came when his back hoof grazed a pole at the double Oxer, and it fell to the ground. All in all, it was an exceptional first show jumping course for the young horse. Westley applauded loudly for her, hoping she placed well. The competition for Emmy was steep.

Emmy rode several horses during the day's show, entering every possible class in show jumping, cross-country, and dressage. She was exhausted by the end of the day, but she couldn't stop to rest. She also had Michelle riding two of the more experienced horses, and her two young Sommer's students. All in all, they all placed highly. Emmy and Thunder placed second overall, and she placed first with Ru in dressage. She hadn't entered the mare in jumping today, feeling she needed more work before that point.

Her students also placed in the top three spots, and Michelle won first in both her classes. Emmy was beaming by the time they loaded their horses up.

"I'd say today was a really good day, overall."

Driving, Westley glanced at Emmy in the passenger seat.

"You looked good out there today. Thunder and the others all did extremely well for their age. You should be proud."

Emmy glanced at the man beside her. She found herself, not for the first time grateful for his presence and support. Smiling at him, she thanked him. Things had been a little awkward between them since the day she had run off, but they were both trying. Emmy had to admit, he was an excellent person to have on the farm. It seemed there was nothing this man couldn't do.

Glancing down at the photo of the newborn Grace she cradled in her lap, Emmy sighed sadly. She had spent so many nights longing for the child she had lost. A warm tear trailed down her cheek as she remembered what it had felt like to hold her tiny baby in her arms. Even after everything she had gone through, Emmy had wanted nothing else except for her baby to survive. No matter how many days or years had gone by, she never seemed to fully get over the loss of her child.

The hurt, the sadness, and the regret was always there. She could not go back, she could not resurrect the child she longed for, but the pain and longing lingered with each passing day. Her heart hadn't healed as others said it would. She would always remember just what that baby smelled like, what she looked like, the tuft of bright red hair upon her head. Feeling the overwhelming emotions hitting her, Emmy stood and placed the photo back onto the mantel. She needed fresh air.

Walking out the French doors leading into the back of the house, Emmy looked up at the large, bright moon above her. Tonight was a full moon. Seemed fitting enough. The air around her was cool, with a mild breeze blowing in. Around her, moonflowers bloomed in their full glory, and the angel's trumpet flowers were still open, allowing their heady fragrance to permeate the air around her.

The silk cream colored nightgown she wore shifted against her body, pulled gently by the breeze. Her mind seemed alive with questions, thoughts, memories as she walked barefoot through the garden she had worked so hard to restore these past few years. Emmy hugged herself, wondering why she still refused to let anyone in, even after all of these years. Was this truly the life she wanted, to be loveless, marriage-less, and childless?

She knew that somewhere deep within herself she still wanted a child of her own. She knew it was highly improbable she would ever have one, but that didn't stop the longing to have one. She had been so sure these past years that she was happy alone, that she need not ever let a man into her life, and then she had met Westley. Having him here on the farm had changed things. She had seen how much it helped to have a strong competent man around, and it left her feeling unsure.

To Emmy, it seemed unusual that she should be in her late twenties, and yet still feel like a teenager when it came to having feelings for a man. She may have grown up and matured, but without any real relationship experience, she knew nothing about how to be with a man, in any sense of the word.

She had dated Leo a handful of times, but she didn't think going to dinner a few times could have prepared her for the whirlwind of emotions she felt around Westley. She was aware of the way he still watched her sometimes when he thought she wasn't paying attention. She had to admit, he fascinated her. With those sultry green eyes and his handsome face, not to even mention his tall strong physique.

Emmy thought it was interesting that she had spent her life around equestrians, and been exposed many times to good-looking men with great bodies, yet not one of them had ever caused her heart to flutter the way Westley did. Just a smile, a wink, any little gesture from the man seemed to send her thoughts to places she didn't even understand. Granted, she knew what sex was and how it worked. She'd realized that during her torture session with Malcolm.

She just wasn't completely sure if it was always supposed to hurt the way it had that night. Pam had told her it did not, and should not ever hurt when you make love with a man who is not forcing you. Still, Emmy wasn't sure she even wanted to think about having a man do things to her ever again. The mere thought caused her to shudder in fear.

Westley paced his room. He'd had another nightmare about the day Joseph died. He couldn't deal with the haunting memories of his brother anymore. He refused to go back to sleep and allow them to overcome his mind. He wanted to remember his brother the way he had been, fun-loving, happy, carefree, not the way he had died.

Pulling on his jeans, and a long sleeve button up flannel, he didn't bother to button the shirt as he stalked from the room. Coming out on the front porch, he ran his fingers through his hair, sighing in exasperation. He didn't want to face the nightmares, and he didn't want to face the horse. Walking around the porch that he realized wrapped around the entire house, he glanced off into the distance, admiring the fullness of the moon.

Something white caught his attention toward the back of the house. Squinting, Westley tried to make out what he was seeing. When it moved slightly, Westley was at first afraid he was seeing a ghost. Walking slowly closer to the garden that sprawled behind the house, he realized it was a woman. Frowning, Westley walked into the garden, determined to figure this mystery out.

As he made his way through the abundant roses and other flowers growing all around him, Westley caught small glimpses of the woman through the foliage. He could see the white or cream color of her dress, but not much more than that. As he peered through the thick plants, not wanting to be a peeping tom, but curious as to who was out here in the middle of the night, he caught sight of the red sheen of her hair, and he realized it was Emmy.

The wind chose that moment to stir the greenery around him. As he watched, Emmy's long loose waves fluttered about her face, and her dress, that he now realized was a very thin nightgown. The dress shifted slightly, hugging every contour, every rise, and dip, every curve of her body, and Westley swallowed. She was breathtaking. He had already known it, but seeing her like this, standing beneath the moonlight with all of her curves visible through the thin silk, Westley realized she was even more beautiful than he had thought.

Realizing he was being a creeper by hiding behind the leaves, Westley made his way around the rose bushes. When he appeared before her, her face went blank, clearly, she had not been expecting him.

"Emmy, I'm sorry to startle you. I saw you from the porch, and I thought I would check on you."

Emmy stared in response for a moment. Blinking, she laughed at herself. "Geez, Westley, I'm sorry, I was off in my own little world I guess."

Smiling, Westley wondered if she was aware of how sheer her nightgown was. He could see practically everything through it, and he immediately regretted coming over to her. The shape of her curves had been hard enough to ignore.

Emmy looked Westley over, instantly becoming aware of his open shirt and exposed chest and abdomen. Her breathing hitched, and her eyes couldn't help but follow the lines of well-defined muscle as they disappeared down into his groin area. Biting her lip, she lifted her face quickly, overwhelmed with the warm tingly sensation that had started in the pit of her stomach. When her eyes sought him, she regretted it immediately.

He was watching her, taking in her reaction to him. She realized he was probably all too aware of how the sight of his skin made her feel. Emmy blinked rapidly. Looking away, she wrapped her arms back across her chest.

"I had a bad night. Couldn't sleep. I was thinking about Grace." Glancing back at Westley again, she asked, "What demons keep you awake at night Westley?"

Westley stared into her deep blue eyes. You. That was what he wanted to say, but instead, he shrugged. "We both seem to be haunted by demons from our past."

Studying his face, Emmy was frustrated. He knew her most vulnerable secret, her darkest nightmare. Yet he was not willing to give her even one detail of his past. It saddened her, and she realized it was just one more hurdle between them. Emmy nodded.

"Well, I should head in. Goodnight Westley." Emmy dropped her gaze, not wanting Westley to see her feelings.

It was too late. Westley had seen it. The moment he finished speaking, he had seen the disappointment, the sadness that crept into her face, and then he had seen the walls go back up. When she turned away from him, Westley threw his head back in frustration. Stepping forward, he touched her arm to stop her.

"Emmy wait." When she turned back to him, it was those damnable eyes of hers that were his undoing. "Please. Don't go. Stay with me, for a little while. Please."

Emmy studied his face. She could see he meant it, he didn't want her to leave. Sighing, she looked away.

"I don't know, Westley, I just don't think it's a good idea."

Westley pulled her all the way up to him until there was only an inch separating them. Emmy's breath caught in her chest. She froze. She was unsure what he was doing, but she couldn't seem to pull away either.

"When are we going to stop pretending that neither of us feel this intense attraction to one another?"

Emmy stuttered. "Westley, I...I uh, I don't know what you're talking about, I don't ...I don't."

Emmy's words went silent when Westley closed the gap between them. With their bodies pressed against each other, she felt like her heart would hammer right out of her chest. Looking up into his green depths, she swallowed.

"Tell me, Emmy. Tell me you don't feel it. Tell me your body does not hunger for mine. Tell me you have not imagined what it would be like to feel my hands on you."

Emmy's voice seemed to have disappeared completely. She cleared her throat several times, trying to ignore the fire igniting inside her everywhere that their bodies touched. She was all too aware of the erratic way her chest rose and fell, only making the connection between their bodies more intense.

Westley grinned. "You can't, can you? You cannot tell me you don't feel it too because you do. I know you went through hell the first time you were with a man, Emmy, but that doesn't mean it has to be that way every time. If you would just stop being so afraid if you would just give us a chance…"

Emmy tried to speak, but when Westley leaned forward and gently touched his lips to hers, all cognitive thought evaporated. The fire in that simple delicate touch was almost too much to bear. Emmy's body responded on its own, not allowing her time to think things through. Leaning into him, she heard herself groan in a husky tone.

Westley, surprised by her sultry response to such a small feather light touch nearly lost it. Leaning into her, he was barely aware of his arms wrapping around her waist and pulling her firmly against him. He wanted her, more than anyone else. He burned with desire for her. Hungered for even the slightest touch.

Emmy's head spun. She had never imagined the feeling of a man's arms around her could feel so good, so right, and so perfect. It didn't even occur to her right then to be afraid. There was nothing in Westley's touch that elicited fear from her. Just need and desire, feelings she had never encountered before.

When Westley deepened the kiss, Emmy's body ignited in a fire, she honestly didn't understand what she was feeling. The way he held her, touched her, kissed her, it was as though this were what she had waited her entire life for. This man, these feelings. Those thoughts terrified her far more than the thought of being with him. Unable to stand the desire any longer, Emmy pulled away. Looking into the intense green of Westley's eyes, she spun on her heels and ran to the house.

Westley felt like hell the following morning. He had lain awake all night, unable to shake the memories of how it had felt to have Emmy pressed against him, the way she tasted, and the incredible ways in which she had responded to him. The other reason he hadn't slept was the fear he had seen in her eyes just before she had fled. He prayed all night that he had not messed things up between the two of them.

Groaning as he crawled out of bed, he decided he needed a very long, very cold shower. He didn't know how much more of this sexual tension he could live through. He did know, however, he was willing to endure this torture as long as it took to gain Emmy's trust.

Rubbing his face as he headed toward the kitchen, feeling slightly better after his cold shower, Westley glanced around the quiet house. There were no signs of Emmy, Greg, or the dogs. Frowning, Westley headed out to the porch, whistling for the pup. He had grown attached to the little collie, and she seemed to have an interest in him as well. Typically, if he whistled for the little Feather, she'd come bounding toward him, letting him know where to find the others.

Today was no exception. The half-grown pup stuck her head out of Emmy's private barn and yipped at him. Westley chuckled. Making his way toward the barn, he had every intention of making sure things were all right between Emmy and him after the previous night. As he made his way toward the barn, he noticed Emmy's truck was missing. The feeling of dread filled the pit of his stomach. Had she run, taken off because of him? Westley clenched his jaw as he rounded the corner of the barn to find Greg mucking Bloodfever's stall.

The deep red chestnut stallion lifted his head, whinnying as he caught the scent of the man he was always looking for. Westley sighed. Would the horse ever stop being so damn attached to him? It was hard enough having the reminder of Joseph's death looking him in the eyes each time he came in this barn, but to have the stallion so actively seek him out, it nearly killed him.

Greg might be young, but he had not missed the exchange between man and horse. No one who saw the pair near each other could miss the connection between these two, but neither could they miss the way Westley struggled to disregard the horse's attachment.

"You know, Westley, I don't know why you dislike this guy, he's so docile, especially for a stallion. Emmy says he has some of the best conformation she has ever seen. I bet he's pretty awesome when he jumps, huh?"

Westley's jaw twitched. "Yeah, sure is kid. Uh, where is Emmy? Her truck is gone. Did she take off?"

Greg frowned at the expression or anxiety on Westley's face.

"I dunno Westley. Did something happen between the two of you to make her run off, again?"

Westley frowned at the way Greg reminded him of the day Emmy had taken off on foot through the pastures.

"No, Greg. Nothing happened."

Greg shrugged, turning back to his chores. "She went to the hospital. Pam went into labor and David called for Emmy to come."

Westley sighed in relief. Then he frowned. Was Emmy ready to be present when a child was born, after what she had gone through? Greg seemed to have read Westley's thoughts as he spoke up.

"I was worried about her going, you know, after Grace and all. Emmy said she would be all right. She said Pam was there for her when Grace was born, so she wouldn't miss this for anything."

Westley nodded. The telephone in the barn started ringing. Thinking it might be Emmy, Westley picked up.

"Hello, Lost Acres Equestrian facility. How can I help you?" Westley thought they had hung up at first.

After the moment of silence, the unmistakable southern drawl came across the line. "Hello. This is Vadetta Everhart, Emmy's mother."

"Hello, Mrs. Everhart. I am afraid Emmy's not here currently. Can I leave her a message?"

"Uh, will she be back soon? I was hoping to talk with her myself."

Westley frowned. "I am honestly not sure. She's at the hospital with Pam."

On the other line, there was a deep intake of breath. "Oh my, is everything ok? Is Pam all right? Is Emmy all right?"

Westley chuckled. "Oh yeah, everyone's fine, well I hope so anyway. Pam went into labor early this morning."

"Oh. Oh I see. Well, that is exciting indeed. Will you tell Emmy I called? Ian was released from the hospital today, and he wanted to make sure she knew."

Westley smiled. "Yes, Ma'am. I will surely tell her as soon as she comes home. Have a good day, Mrs. Everhart."

Hanging up the receiver, Westley lifted his brows at Greg. "Well, I guess we had better get working."

Grinning with too much enthusiasm for Westley's security, Greg shrugged.

"Yep. Ought to be an interesting day, Emmy said you will be in charge of giving lessons today."

Westley groaned. He really was in no mood to deal with spoiled children and their spoiled mothers.

∞∞∞∞

-*8*-

Watching Pam give birth to her son was harder than Emmy had ever thought possible. Seeing David there beside her, being the amazing husband he was, made it all the more bittersweet for Emmy. She was overjoyed with happiness for her friend, and she wished the bitterness didn't creep its ugly head inside of her, but she wasn't able to fully control her feelings.

The labor lasted twenty-two hours, and Pam had committed herself to delivering without an epidural or medications of any kind. That was a part of it Emmy did was not envious about. When the baby was born, all nine pounds of him, Emmy smiled with delight. He was red-faced and coated with fluids. With his full head of thick dark hair, he definitely resembled his mother and not the fair complexioned David.

Pam had been overwrought with emotions throughout the entire morning, and when they laid her son on her chest, she burst into sobs. Emmy knew it was tears of happiness that clogged her eyes. The baby, they named

Christopher David Ryans. Emmy hugged her friend, congratulating her on the successful birth of her healthy baby boy. After delivering a bouquet of flowers and a soft blue teddy bear tied to balloons to the new mother's room, Emmy showed herself out, allowing the two of them to be alone with their precious gift.

In the parking lot outside the hospital, Emmy cried for nearly an hour. Some were happy tears and some sad. She had been reminded so much of baby Grace as she had watched her friends baby boy be born. She felt like her heart had been torn open again. She heaved in a deep breath of air as she tried to work through the pain. She really didn't think she would ever get through it.

Today, Emmy told herself. Today was the day she would catch Southern Wind. A few weeks had gone by since she had taken Fio away from him for her breeding, and although he had been extremely displeased at first, he had settled down after a while and had not bolted. After the mare had been taken, Emmy had noticed the colt display a more intense interest in her. He now allowed her to approach him, to feed him grain from a bucket, and on occasion to brush him.

So today, she told herself she would test the tentative bond they had been slowly building. She tossed a halter and lead rope over her shoulder, and placed a crop in her back pocket, just in case the colt became too aggressive. So far, he had displayed no signs of aggression with her. He showed fear, but not aggression. Emmy hoped she would have no need of the crop for she feared it would set them back, but she knew she also didn't need a broken leg.

Picking up her grain bucket, she began the long walk to the pasture where the colt stayed. There were horses on either side of him, and he seemed content enough with that. As she approached the gate, the dark colt lifted his head, twitched his ears, and neighed softly. Emmy smiled. Calling a greeting to the horse, she entered the gate.

Things were going well after a few minutes. The colt happily munched grain from the bucket on the ground, and Emmy gently stroked his neck with her hands. Slowly, she replaced one hand with the lead line. The colt flinched at the difference in material but ignored it otherwise. After spending a few minutes rubbing him with the rope, placing it around his neck, she removed the halter and began the slow, steady introduction toward his face.

A few times, the colt jerked his head away, but the grain kept his attention enough for Emmy to continue. Slowly, she maneuvered the opening of the halter into the grain bucket, allowing the colt to sniff it, and become acquainted with the foreign object. When he seemed to be comfortable with it, Emmy slipped it over the bridge of his dark nose, past the streak of gray, and fastened it behind his ears.

The colt lifted his head, snorted, and shook his head. Lifting the grain bucket, Emmy gave it a shake, gaining his attention. Slowly, she walked around the pasture with the grain bucket in one hand, and the lead line in the other. The colt could feel the weight of the halter, could feel the slight pressure of the lead when Emmy changed directions, but he stayed calm and focused on getting his grain.

Emmy grinned. Things had gone much better than she had expected. The colt had not initially liked the feeling of the halter or the pressure of the lead, but he was slowly learning to trust her. He also really liked his grain. After the grain had all been eaten down, Emmy spent another hour with the colt, leading him and getting him used to the feel of the halter and what the different pressures meant. All in all, it had been a great day.

When she exited the pasture, she found Westley watching her. He was propped up with one shoulder leaning casually against the post. He grinned at her as she approached him.

"Hey, beautiful. That's a mighty fine colt you have there. This is, I'm assuming the special one right?"

Ignoring his first comment, although it was difficult, Emmy nodded.

"Yeah, this is the one I have big hopes for. He's had a bit of a rough start, but I think he has the potential to be even better than View."

Westley cocked a brow. "Wow. Those are powerful words. Better than Viewfinder? I don't think I have even seen his equal."

Emmy knew she shouldn't go there, but she couldn't stop herself. "What about Fever? From what you've said he was in line to be the top of his class."

Westley frowned. Emmy watched his expression darken. "Westley, if you don't trust me, then how do you expect me to learn to trust you?"

Westley's jaw ticked. "I told you, Emmy. It's not about trusting you. It's about the past, and what we should drudge up and what we should not. If I hadn't gone with you that night to see your brother, do you honestly think you would have volunteered the information to me yourself?"

Emmy shrugged. Walking past Westley, she held her chin up in defiance.

"I don't know, Westley, in all probability, no, I'm sure I would not have, but you speak of wanting more from me, and I'm not willing to give it to a man who will not trust me with his demons."

Watching her head to the barn, Westley growled. She was infuriating sometimes. Leaning on the fence, he watched the almost completely black colt as it watched Emmy. The colt couldn't have cared less about the man, and Westley found that humorous. Here they were, both privately infatuating over the same woman.

Pam grinned at her husband. They had just pulled down the long drive that wound toward Lost Acres, and she was excited to see her friend.

"David, I did mention she had hired that reporter as her barn manager, didn't I?"

David smiled at her, then frowned. "Reporter? You mean the one that came out and wrote that article a few years ago? How did he go from being a reporter to a hand here?"

Grinning, Pam told him the story Emmy had given her about how and why Westley Galway had ended up working on their farm.

When she was done, David glanced at her, and asked, "I can see you are elated about this situation. Is there a reason?"

Pamela Ryans smiled mischievously at her husband. Squeezing his hand in fondness, she replied, "Ask me that again after we've been here an hour, love."

Hearing the truck pull down the drive, Emmy grinned at Greg.

"Alright kid, here comes Pam, David, and little Christopher, so your mom and dad should be here soon. You've been here four months now, I hope you're ready to show them what an amazing young man you have become."

Greg, embarrassed by the sentiment in Emmy's eyes, fixed his shirt and nodded. Mumbling something about checking dinner, he retreated post-haste into the house.

Emmy laughed. Watching the boy go into the house, she smiled. She had come to care a great deal for the boy who was quickly becoming a young man. Glancing toward the private barn where she kept the stallions, Emmy sighed. Westley had been in a mood all morning. He had been scrubbing every inch of that barn, and yet still managing to avoid the one horse who was devoted to the man.

"Emmy, dear, why the pensive look? You're supposed to be overjoyed with happiness to see your best friend."

Turning, Emmy pulled Pam into a tight hug. "Oh, I am overjoyed to see you, I just have a lot on my mind today."

Pamela studied her. Lifting a brow in amusement, she asked, "That something wouldn't happen to have an Irish accent and a roguishly handsome smile, would it?"

Emmy laughed while sending Pam an amused expression. "Let's not even go there. We can talk about anything but that."

Catching sight of David bringing the car seat and baby around, Emmy grinned.

"Awe, I get to see my Godson again. How's parenthood treating you, Pammy? You look great, even just a week after the birth."

Pam grinned, and the light in her eyes was obvious. She was glowing from the inside out. It was obvious being a mother suited her.

"It's amazing, Emmy. I mean, I'm exhausted, but it's so worth it. David is such a big help too, and little Topher is such a good baby."

David smiled at Emmy. "Hey, sweetheart. How have you been? Did your crazy friend tell you she bought him a riding helmet already?"

Laughing, Emmy looked at Pam in question. She was immediately aware of the moment when Westley walked up on the porch, and she tried her hardest not to acknowledge him.

"You didn't? Where did you even find one small enough for his tiny head? Oh my goodness, it must be so cute!"

Westley nodded at David. "Mr. Ryans, how are you? I hear congratulations are in order."

Turning toward Pam, he continued, "Mrs. Ryans, you are as lovely as ever."

David grinned proudly. Lifting the soft blue blanket from the infant seat, he put his finger to his lips. "Little guy's worn himself out."

Peeking into the carrier, Westley smiled. The boy looked just like his mom. His dark hair was incredibly thick already, and his skin tone had the same olive hue of Pam. He was a big healthy baby. Glancing up at the pair of them, he nodded.

"He's quite a looker. I'll bet he'll keep the two of you busy."

Turning to see Emmy standing slightly behind Pam, Westley tried to keep his voice and face neutral.

"Evening, Emmy. That barn darn near sparkles now. I had better go clean up and leave you all to your get-together."

Emmy, spurred by surprise that Westley assumed he was not invited, acted upon instinct without thinking first.

Reaching out, she lightly touched his arm. "Westley, you are invited too. Actually, I'm pretty sure you're expected to be there."

The two held each other's gaze for a long moment, forgetting about the other couple beside them.

"All right, Emmy. If you're sure, I'd be happy to join you all. I'll just go clean up and I'll be out in a bit."

Pam watched Westley disappear into the house. Glancing at her husband, she lifted her brow at his shocked expression. Sidling up to him as Emmy walked out to meet the Fitzgerald car as it pulled up, she lowered her voice.

"Well, darling, what do you think?"

"What do I think? You said an hour. We've been here less than ten minutes, and already I can slice clean through the sexual tension between those two. More than that though, it's not just sexual tension I sense. There is something more profound, deeper, and emotional. Damn. You were right, baby. Maybe this Irishman is good for her."

Pamela Ryans grinned mischievously. "Oh, I think he would be really good for her. He is, after all, the first man I have seen her react to like this."

Emmy laughed at Rae Fitzgerald. She had yet to stop thanking Emmy for the transition in her son. The boy she had sent here seemed to have been replaced by a young man with polite manners and apparent love for cooking.

"Seriously Emmy, I cannot believe what you have done. Please, you have to tell me what your secret is."

Emmy laughed. "Well, scrubbing mats we use in the breeding shed seems to make a big impression on him. Ever since I used that as a punishment, he certainly thinks twice before acting out."

Rae stared at Emmy in horror for a moment. Emmy was uncertain about her friend's reaction when Rae let loose a stream of laughter.

Beside her, her husband Michael shook his head. "Oh, Emmy, that's rich!"

Emmy's body buzzed with excitement as she watched Westley enter the dining room. He had showered, shaved, and donned a new looking pair of dark jeans, and a deep gray button up that seemed to complement and bring out his green eyes. With his longish hair falling slightly above his brows, he looked sexy as ever.

Westley's eyes found Emmy standing near the far side of the dining table, and he nearly tripped. She had dressed up in a knee-length black dress that hugged her curves and showed off her shoulders. The sight of so much of her golden-toned skin visible nearly undid him. Her rich auburn hair hung in long loose waves down her back, and she'd even applied a touch of makeup. She didn't need it. Westley thought she was beautiful with it, but she was just as lovely without it.

Their eyes seemed to seek each other out immediately. The intensity of their locking gaze was not lost on anyone in the room. Westley, aware they were being watched by several people, broke the contact and walked toward the champagne bar that had been set up. He eyed the bottle, then walked away. That stuff had done nothing but get him in trouble lately.

Pam had watched the intense connection between the two as their gazes had held. She had no doubt this was the man for her Emmy. Now, she just needed to figure out how to get the two to let their guard down long enough for them to figure that out. Smiling to herself as she plotted the romance she could see blossoming, she plucked a glass of champagne from the tray and headed to her best friend.

Holding it out to Emmy, she smiled and winked. "Have a glass with me love, as a toast for the amazing year we have been having."

Eyeing the offered glass as well as the one in Pam's hand, Emmy cocked a brow in suspicion. "Pam, aren't you breast-feeding?"

Swirling the glass in question, she grinned. "Apple cider darling. The next best thing." The two shared a laugh.

"You know I don't hold my alcohol very well, Pammy. The champagne is for my guests. I get a little tipsy quickly, you know that."

Precisely. Pam smiled innocently. "Oh, come now Emmy, just one glass. Amongst friends you have nothing to worry about."

Emmy eyed her friend with suspicion. Taking the offered glass, she narrowed her eyes.

"I have known you since we were ten. Don't think I cannot see a plot when it's in your mind, Pammy. Whatever you're thinking, or planning, just don't, ok."

With her tinkling laugh, Pam shrugged her shoulders and sent Emmy a baffled look. Inside, she was cheering as Emmy swallowed her first sip of the heady champagne. Across the room, Pam could easily see the way Westley had a hard time focusing on the conversation with Michael and David as his eyes seemed to constantly seek Emmy out. Oh yeah, Pam thought this had to be the chance for Emmy she had been waiting for.

Throughout the meal, Emmy tried her best to ignore the way her body seemed drawn to Westley. She tried to ignore him completely. It was much harder than she ever would have imagined. Every time he laughed, the deep baritone of his voice sent shivers down her spine. When his conversation drifted to her ears periodically, she found herself straining to listen, to hear the words he said, hoping for any little detail about this man.

Emmy hadn't realized she was into her third glass of champagne until it was too late. She could hear herself giggle with Pam and Rae, but the sound didn't quite penetrate the fog of her mind. She felt the flush in her cheeks, but she told herself she was just happy to be gathered with her close friends.

Across the room, Westley tried to keep his breathing even, and his composure cool. He truly enjoyed talking with Emmy's friends, and could easily picture himself as their friend, but the way Emmy's eyes sought him out, the way her faced flushed and the sound of her soft laughter drifting to his ears throughout the night was straining every ounce of control he had. He wanted her badly. Needed her with a desperation that was incredibly unlike him.

Half the time, he couldn't even recall the words the other two men had said to him only seconds before. Worse, was when the two men caught him watching her as they awaited his reply in the conversation. Westley felt like a wreck. If he didn't put some distance between himself and the sensual redhead soon, the consequences could be disastrous.

He needed to leave, to get out, to be away from Emmy for the night, or he was going to lose his mind and make a mistake that could wind up costing him big time where she was concerned. He might know what he wanted, but he knew Emmy did not. She was not ready for the intensity of his feelings. She needed someone who could control themselves, not a man who was no better than an oversexed teenager.

Emmy heard Westley excuse himself, saying he had plans to meet up with a friend tonight. Her heart dropped at his words. The disappointment hit her harder than she would have expected as she watched him head to his room. Beside her, Pam was frowning deeply. Emmy, unsure of what came over her at that moment, excused herself.

Standing just outside Westley's door, Emmy fidgeted with her hands. Why was she here? What was she planning to say, to do? She had no clue what she was thinking. About to abandon her attempt, Emmy had just turned away when Westley's door opened, and a surprised Westley stood before her.

"Emmy, I didn't hear you knock. What are you doing here? Did you need me to do something before I head out?"

Westley's heart beat frantically at the sight of a flushed Emmy standing outside his door.

"Uh, actually, I hadn't yet knocked. I was just about to, but then you came out. Can I... uh, can I have a word with you?"

Westley nodded, but when Emmy glanced toward his room, and he realized she wanted to speak with him inside, he nearly stopped breathing. His bedroom was most definitely not an ideal place to have a conversation with the object of his lust. How could he refuse? Westley began to nod, about to pretend he hadn't understood her message, but apparently, Emmy misread his reaction. Smiling, she stepped past him, right into the worst place for her to be.

Glancing around his room, Emmy tried to calm her heart. She wasn't sure what she was doing, asking to speak with him in his room, or for that matter, even what she needed to speak to him about. Once she had entered his domain, she regretted it immediately. The room may have been clean and orderly, but it literally breathed his scent. Everything in here reminded her of the big attractive man, and the result was a heightened sexual awareness of him she didn't know how to react to.

She glanced at his bed, then closed her eyes briefly, realizing immediately her mistake as foreign images played out in her mind of a naked Westley. Whoa. Taking a deep breath, she quickly turned away. Seeing the photo of a young man seated atop Bloodfever, with Westley standing beside the horse, Emmy stepped forward for a closer look. Before she could see much more, Westley deftly laid the photo face down.

"Emmy. You wanted to speak to me privately. What's wrong? What is it you needed?"

Emmy could sense Westley urge to get her out of his room. Had she read him wrong, had she felt all these emotions for a man who was not interested in her? Her mind spun with question after question. Did he have someone else? She felt like she was making herself into a fool for nothing.

"Uh, well, I uh…" Staring at Westley, looking into his mesmerizing green eyes with the champagne heavily impairing her judgment, Emmy sighed. What the hell. One step forward, and she crashed roughly into Westley's chest. Looking up at his surprised expression, she leaned up on her tiptoes, pressing her lips to his.

Westley groaned. Desire coursed through him with a vengeance. His first reaction was to grab Emmy around the waist and crush her against him, chasing away any space that tried to come between them. With her body in full contact with him, and her lips devouring his, Westley ran his hands down her back, pressing into her.

Emmy gasped as sensations coursed through her body everywhere that their bodies touched. She was overcome with a need she didn't know nor understand. She wanted this man. She knew that without doubt. What she didn't know, however, was if she was ready for that. Her body told her she most definitely was, but her mind held back.

Westley nearly lost his control. Lifting Emmy, he shifted her until her legs went around his waist, and her arms wove behind his neck. He felt her hesitate at first, but as he deepened the kiss, she relaxed against him. With his hands holding firmly to the delicious curve of her thighs, Westley thought he was going to lose his mind. Pressing Emmy to the wall behind them, he just about lost himself.

Emmy's body was on fire. She wanted him to touch her, to kiss her more. She wanted to trust this man, to erase the memory of another with him. With the feel of his rough hands on her thighs, she felt like she was going to explode. When the hardness of him pressed against her most sacred place, she froze. All the feelings that had been assaulting her came to an immediate halt. Images of that day came flooding back to her, and Emmy felt her chin tremble. Pulling away from his kiss, she pushed him away.

She couldn't get away from him fast enough. Tears stung her eyes, and her legs threatened to give out from beneath her. She began hyperventilating. Westley froze, his body hard with need, his mind spinning, trying to recover from the haze of lust she had put him in. He knew she was freaking out, and he knew why, but at that moment, he didn't know how to help her. His thoughts deserted him, and his conscience got the better of him.

Gritting his teeth, Westley swore. "This is never going to happen again, Emmy."

Westley tore out of the room and left the house. He didn't want to face the people gathered there, probably wondering where Emmy had gone. Westley berated himself as he fled the farm. He was an idiot. He shouldn't have left, but once he had, he couldn't seem to stop himself. He had messed up. He should have been in control of the situation. He didn't know why he couldn't seem to get ahold of himself when he was around her.

Emmy sat on the porch chair staring into the dark. The last thing she had wanted that night was to be alone, and yet here she was, with only her dogs to keep her company in the looming silence of the sprawling ranch house. The quite seemed to be everywhere. Greg had gone with his parents for the weekend, and when all the goodbyes had been said, Emmy found herself utterly alone.

She had always been okay with alone. She was used to being by herself, but now, she didn't want to be with her thoughts. It had been hard enough gaining control of her emotions after Westley had taken off, but putting on a smile for her friends had nearly undone her. She was aware of the way Pam watched her, worrying about her, and she could tell her friend hadn't wanted to leave.

Emmy was ashamed of herself. She had acted like a common whore, and look what it had gotten her. She had run Westley off with her issues, and now here she sat, feeling vulnerable, and unwanted. He had responded to her kiss much more ardently than she had expected. Who was she kidding? She had responded like a wild hormonal teenager. Until that moment when their bodies had touched in that intimate area, and she had freaked out.

She was a freak. There was no arguing against it. She was a freak. A grand disaster. She couldn't even be physical with a man. Could hardly allow them to touch her. She had, she realized, wanted Westley to touch her. Badly. Her feelings for the man had grown more and more by the day, and here she was, playing the fool.

Standing, Emmy entered the house. When she passed through the dining area to begin cleaning up, she picked up the champagne bottle to throw it away. Stopping when she realized the bottle was nearly full, Emmy glanced down at it. Should she save it? Why? No one here would drink it. Might as well toss it. As she headed to the sink to pour the heady stuff out, she pictured the horrified expression on Westley's face as he'd turned away from her.

Emmy faltered. She stood, staring at the sink for several moments as the tears flowed down her face. She was irrevocably screwed up. She might as well face it, the only thing she was ever going to be good at was riding horses. Turning, she walked absently back to the porch. Plopping down in the chair as a sob tore from her chest, Emmy put the champagne bottle to her lips. What the hell. Why shouldn't she drown her sorrow in alcohol? She was going to spend the rest of her life alone, without ever knowing what it really meant to love and make love to a man.

The problem with drinking was not the one bottle of champagne. It was the nearly three bottles that lay on the porch as Emmy stood, wobbly but capable of walking. Her eyes focused on the barn in the distance. She stood, neither blinking nor moving. Seemingly unbidden, her legs lead her away from the porch. She didn't completely realize where she was going or what she was doing until she stood, staring through the filmy darkness at the bloody-colored horse.

Even in the darkness, his big dark soulful eyes watched her. Emmy swayed. She looked deep into the eyes of Westley's horse, for she knew him to be that. This horse belonged to Westley, heart, and soul. Just like her. She didn't know where the thought had come from, but she didn't care at this point. Stepping forward, she entered the stall. Running her fingers softly over the sleek satin coat of the blood-red stallion, Emmy allowed herself to clear her mind.

The stallion was aware of her, his ears twitched, his eyes followed her. As her hands touched his back, his shoulders, his neck, she allowed herself to communicate silently with the animal, to learn him. Then, Emmy hoisted herself up onto the horse's back. Sitting astride the wide barreled Irish Warmblood stallion, Emmy breathed deeply the scent of horse.

The smell calmed her, reeling her emotions in, and centering her. It was the only thing that ever had. Still in her black dress, she sat with her bare thighs pressing against the strong back of the horse. Her dress hiked up around her thighs, and the result was a connection unhindered by saddle or material.

She could feel the stallion's body respond to her, attuning itself to her, waiting for her cues. Leaning forward, Emmy pushed the door to the stall open and applied gentle pressure as she guided the horse from its stall. Without any device marring the majestic beauty of the horse, Emmy sat astride the big animal. The horse offered no hesitation. He responded to Emmy's commands as though the two had been built from one cloth.

Emmy closed her eyes momentarily as the tears flowed again. This horse, the way he moved, the way he responded to her every thought, how could Westley ignore such a creature? This horse had clearly been trained extremely well. The willingness to please his rider alone was sentiment to a perfect horse.

Heading into the indoor arena, Emmy still could not believe this docile intelligent stallion did as asked without any halter, any rope, anything. She thought it, he reacted. It was truly that simple, and that perfect. He read every cue from her body with perfection. Again Emmy was hit with images of Westley and her clouded mind struggled to stay focused. The way his hands had felt, the intensity of those eyes.

Another sob escaped her chest as Emmy tried to push thoughts of him from her mind. She had ruined any chance she had with the man. Leaning forward slightly,

Emmy asked the horse for a canter. The horse transitioned smoothly into a canter. The motion was graceful, smooth, collected. Again Emmy was overjoyed with the feel of the animal. This horse was a masterpiece.

The motion sensing lights had kicked on when she entered the arena, and Emmy's mind fought the fog of the champagne. She wanted, needed to feel the wind around her. She needed to fly. Asking the horse toward one of the jumps lined up in the center of the arena, Emmy inhaled deeply as she asked him forward. Without the slightest refusal, the horse few over the two-foot jump.

The momentum was perfect. The footing, the leap, the landing. Perfect. Emmy felt tears well from her eyes. How? How could Westley lock this horse away and ignore him? This horse was perfection itself. Emmy felt the sensation of flying as she cleared another jump. Again the horse executed it perfectly.

Westley parked his truck. Running his finger through his hair, he sighed. Sitting at the bar counter alone had done little to dispel the sense of loss Westley felt. Why he couldn't just control himself around one red-haired woman, he just didn't know. The one glass of Irish whiskey he'd allowed himself to indulge in hadn't helped. Instead of chasing away his demons, it had brought them closer.

Stepping up onto the porch, Westley was surprised to see the door still open. He nearly tripped on the champagne bottle he had failed to see. Cursing, he glanced down at the three bottles strewn about. Frowning, Westley glanced around. Noticing the light coming from the arena, his frown deepened.

"Please tell me she didn't get drunk and decide to go riding. Is she trying to kill herself?" Westley sighed.

He hadn't wanted to face Emmy right now, but it looked like he had no choice. Rubbing his face, he walked toward the arena. As he neared the open door, he caught a streak of red out of the corner of his eyes. That color, that red.

Opening his eyes wide, Westley sprinted the rest of the way. He prayed he was wrong. He prayed the woman wasn't foolish enough to be riding the horse he feared. Stopping short at the gate that hung wide open, Westley swallowed as he stared at the sight that greeted him. Emmy rode Bloodfever with neither saddle nor bridle. Her dress was hitched up around her hips, and they flew over the four-foot rail. With his heart stopping, Westley shook his head. Ahead of the pair, a jump had been assembled to simulate the cross-country four-foot parallel over four-foot of water.

Westley's stomach dropped. No. Not that one. Westley stood frozen in fear as the pair galloped toward the jump. If he reacted now, the horse could spook and that would be even worse. He waited in fearful silence for the catastrophe to happen. Emmy was perfect. Perfect form, perfect control. She clung to the horse, leaning forward at the optimal time. The horse was perfect. He never hesitated as he flew through the air over the wide jump, landing with not one mishap.

Westley couldn't believe what he was seeing. There had been no hesitation, no refusal, and no accident where Emmy flew through the air over the jump as his brother had. The whole thing played through his mind over and over. He didn't understand. Why had the stallion done it without a stitch of tack for a woman who had never ridden him before, but he had refused his own rider that day five years earlier.

Coming out of his haze, Westley stepped angrily into the arena. Without thinking, he bellowed Emmy's name as he strode toward her. Emmy twisted toward him in surprise as the horse galloped past him. The movement caused her to lose her balance, sending her flying off the back of the horse. Westley felt the blood drain from his face as he watched her fall through the air and land in a heap on the sandy arena floor.

Leaping toward her at the same time as the horse wheeled around to stand beside the woman, Westley prayed fervently she wasn't hurt, or worse.

"Emmy! Emmy! Please, can you hear me?"

Gently, Westley inspected Emmy where she lay, afraid to move her. He felt her pulse and saw her chest rise and fall. Grateful, he threw his head back and caught sight of the stallion leaning over her. His rage at the animal's betrayal flared to life, fueled by the whiskey and shock of seeing Emmy fall. Lunging toward the horse, he glared.

"You stupid animal! Will you kill her, too? All of that training, all of that time, and all you're good for is ruining people's lives! I should have shot you when I had the chance!"

Emmy pulled herself up, groaning from the surprise impact into the coarse sand. She spat sand from her mouth, sure she had it everywhere. Pulling herself up, she watched Westley wave his arms at the horse frantically, chasing the horse that refused to run. Feeling angry for being surprised right off the horse, and angry for the way Westley acted toward the animal when it was his own fault she'd fallen, Emmy stood and stormed toward him.

"I put everything I had into you! I picked you out because you were going to be a champion! I trusted you! My own brother! You goddamned bloody horse! I should have known all you'd bring was death! God! Joseph! Why him? Why didn't you just take the damn jump?"

Emmy came to an abrupt halt. Joseph? Who was that? What was Westley yelling about? Was he drunk? Stalking forward, Emmy yelled at him.

"Leave the bloody horse alone, Westley! You're the one who made me fall, coming in here yelling! Who the hell are you rattling on about, you damn fool?"

Whirling around, Westley examined the disheveled appearance of the woman. Her deep red hair was a disaster, and her damn dress was clinging to the tops of her hips, revealing an all too tantalizing view of her sexy black lace underwear. A sheen of sand coated her legs and arms, and he could already see the bruises forming on her. Worse, she was pissed.

Westley stared at her. He had never wanted anything more in his life than he wanted her now. The very thought made him angry. He wanted her after she had ridden his horse without his consent. Glaring at her, he ignored her question.

"Where the hell do you get off riding my horse, Emmy? Not just my horse, but a horse I've made it clear no one was to ride?"

Glaring right back at him, Emmy placed her hands on her hips, oblivious to the fact that her torso was completely exposed. "How dare you! Why can't you answer me, Westley? Who is Joseph and why do you hate this horse who is like perfection?"

"Joseph is none of your damn business Emmy, and neither is this horse or the reason I don't like him! You could have been killed."

Emmy laughed. "Are you serious? I've taken more risks in the show ring, harder falls, and on horses with half the training this one has. If you'd not have come bellowing like some drunken fool..."

"Drunken fool! Hah! Says the one who leaves bottles all over the porch like an alcoholic! Don't you know how dangerous it is to ride when you've been drinking?"

Emmy stared daggers at him. "Of course I know that. If you hadn't had to ruin the night by storming out, maybe I wouldn't have drank!"

Westley stared at Emmy. Was she implying she had indulged because he had left her after their encounter? "What?"

Emmy felt herself tremble with anger. "Why did you have to walk out Westley? Did you finally give up and decide I'm too screwed up to waste your time on? Fed up with not getting the sex you want because I'm too damn messed up?"

Westley inhaled deeply. He could feel the anger subsiding from him, and he could see that in retrospect, Emmy's ire was only getting started. Now that the hot Irish temper was cooling, Westley could see Emmy's red puffy eyes and the tear stains that still stuck to her cheeks. The reality that he had affected her so much, rather than pushing her away as he had feared hit him hard in the gut.

Taking a step forward, he sighed. "Emmy..."

Emmy shook her head. Taking a step back, she practically spat at him. "No, don't you dare come near me after running out on me, and then scaring me off that damn horse, not to mention..."

Westley pulled the angry beautiful woman into his arms. Leaning down, he looked into her emotional blue eyes. "Emmy, shut up."

Enraged, Emmy tried to pull away. "Shut up! How dare..."

Her words were silenced when Westley pressed his warm soft lips down on hers. Emmy's body went limp. Westley didn't care anymore. He didn't care how mad she got, how scared. He was going to win this spitfire over if it were the last thing he ever did. Scooping her up into his arms, eliciting a shriek from Emmy, Westley proceeded to carry her to the house.

Emmy argued the entire time. Struggling to get down, but Westley had an iron grip on her. Looking down into her eyes, he sighed.

"Emmy, stop fighting me. I'm not letting you go."

Emmy didn't want to explore the different meanings his statement could have. "Westley Galway put me down. I am more than capable of walking."

Grinning, Westley gave a shake of his head. "If I put you down you might hit me. Besides, then I don't get to feel those lovely thighs."

With her face flaring red, Emmy glared. "I'm going to hit you if you don't put me down now Westley!"

Emmy hadn't realized Westley had stepped into her room until he leaned over, gently placing her on her bed. Emmy started to pull away when she realized Westley didn't appear to be letting go. She watched in trepidation as he leaned over her, kissing her soundly.

"Emmy, you are covered in sand, and you're going to be sore as hell in the morning. Take a warm bath, and get some sleep."

Emmy's jaw dropped as she watched him exit and close her door. If he wasn't the most infuriating man she had ever met! Telling her what she should or should not do. Standing, Emmy had every intention of storming to his room and hitting him square in his handsome jaw. Yanking her door open, Emmy found Westley leaning on the door frame.

"Emmy, if you don't take yourself to the bath right now, I might just be tempted to wash you myself."

Emmy felt her face turn bright red. "You wouldn't dare." Slamming the door in his face, Emmy seethed her entire way to the bathtub, because she had no doubt he would dare.

∞∞∞∞

-9-

Through the week that had followed her fall from Blood fever, Emmy had been incredibly sore. She was grateful she hadn't injured more than just her pride. To say things had been tedious between her and Westley would have been an understatement. She wished the horse wasn't such a touchy subject with Westley because she could hardly think of anything but riding that horse.

Instead, she put her everything into working with Wind. He had a long way to go from the ten-year-old stallion Fever was, but she knew this colt had it in him to be a force to reckon with. The trust between them was growing, and during the week that had followed her reckless night, she had advanced with him in great strides. Now, he met her willingly at the gate and even tolerated the halter without the incentive of grain.

From the gate, Pam called out to her. "Wow, Emmy. I cannot believe you have actually managed to catch that wild beast. He's one fine looking horse. I cannot wait to see you ride him."

Laughing, Emmy released the colt from his lesson on lounging and patted him soothingly. Walking towards the gate, she shrugged. "He's got a long way to go before we get there, I'm afraid. I doubt we'll be seeing any shows for a few years too. He needs to be ready, and learn not to be so afraid."

Lifting a brow, Pam intertwined her arm with Emmy's as they headed toward the barn. "Speaking of not being afraid...any progress with Westley?"

Frowning, Emmy sent her friend a bemused look. "What are you talking about Pam? What about Westley?"

"Oh, don't be coy with me Emmy. You know very well what I'm talking about. The two of you are so hot for one another, no one can miss it."

Emmy shook her head. Opening her mouth to argue and deny it, she looked at her friend, paused, and blew out her breath.

"There's no use denying it with you, Pammy. You know me too well. I don't know what to do about Westley. I... I think I'm ....well, I care for him a lot, and yes, there is definitely an attraction there, but I always ruin things, and I sense there are things from his past that haunt him and...."

Looking into Pam's face, Emmy burst into laughter. "Oh, I'm totally screwed aren't I, Pammy?"

Laughing and feeling sympathetic for her friend, Pam shrugged. "Depends. How have things been going between you two?"

Emmy didn't really want to divulge any details with even Pam, but truth be told, she needed some advice.

"We, uh...we've kissed a few times...and uh, we've argued a couple times... and then there was that time we practically ended up in bed together, but then I freaked out, and I well you know."

Pam had stopped walking and stared at her friend in disbelief.

"Wow. You've done things together...you, Emmy Everhart? Damn girl, this guy really must be something special. So, what's holding you back Emmy?"

Emmy gaped at her. "Seriously Pam? What's holding me back? Oh, gee, first of all, I'm terrified, secondly, I'm not going to just sleep around."

Pam studied her friend for a long time. "In life, many people go a long time before they find the one for them. Sometimes, you have relationships with sex and all, and it doesn't work out. Emmy, I think there are things far worse in this world than you overcoming your fear of sex with a man like Westley, no matter if you end up soul mates or not."

Emmy frowned. "I guess I'm old fashioned and it doesn't feel right thinking about having sex with a man that's not my husband."

Pam sighed heavily. She wanted to advise her friend the right way. "Emmy. Follow your heart. If it feels right to you, then go for it. If it doesn't, then take it slow. You are the only one who knows your own heart."

Watching the two women walk and laugh together, Westley continued mucking the stall he was working on. Across from him, Bloodfever nickered, trying to get his attention. Looking skyward, Westley wished his mother were here to advise him. He needed help. He didn't know what to do about Emmy and ignoring the horse he had loved was getting harder and harder on him.

He felt sure that were his mother still here, she would know what to do. She had always known what to do. Thinking back to the last day she had been alive, Westley recalled her words.

"Go to America, my son, make that woman fall in love with you. Live your life. And forgive him."

Feeling the sting of emotions, Westley sighed. He had little doubt his mother had been talking about the horse. He had every intention of winning Emmy over, it just wasn't all that easy. The woman was stubborn. She had avoided him with a polite professional attitude all week.

He was tempted to lock her in his room with him just to force a reaction from her.

Pam and Emmy made their way toward him, and he had to admit he was grateful for Pam. She always seemed to bring out the happy side of Emmy, to remind her not to work too hard, and to enjoy life. She was a one of a kind friend, and Westley couldn't imagine Emmy having faced her past without someone as good as Pam.

The phone rang, and Emmy ran to get it. Although Westley couldn't hear the words she spoke, he could tell she wasn't altogether happy about the conversation. Coming out of the stall, he pushed the wheelbarrow past her, nodding at Pam, and winking at Emmy. When her face flushed, he grinned.

Hanging up the phone, Emmy rubbed her temples. Beside her, Pam stood with her eyebrows lifted in curiosity.

"What was that Emmy? Let me guess, it was your family. You only get that expression on your face when it has to do with one of them."

Emmy laughed. "It was Ian. He wants to come for a visit. I don't know if I'm completely ready for all of that."

Pam considered this for a minute. "You know Emmy, I cannot help wondering, would a relationship with Westley be easier if you were able to forgive your family, to repair that part of your hurt."

Emmy shrugged. "I don't know Pam." Effectively changing the subject, Emmy said, "Oh, by the way, one of the women who takes lessons is a correctional officer for the local youth division, and she wanted me to consider taking on some kids from the program that is trying to get kids out of trouble. I think she called it Y.W.T.B.B.F. Youth Working To Build Better Futures. I told her I would speak to you about it because this center belongs to both of us."

Pam wasn't too fond of her changing the subject, but she considered Emmy's words.

"You know, that wouldn't be a bad thing, as long as we keep the numbers small so we can keep an eye on them. I'd be down for it. Now that I'm not a whale, I plan to come out at least two to three times a week, take on more students, and help you out a bit more."

Emmy grinned. "It would be great to see more of you, but are you sure you're ready to be away from Topher already?"

"Away from him? No way. I figured I would set up a nursery area in the office and hire someone who could keep an eye on him while I'm out here. That way I can still breastfeed too."

Emmy smiled. "That sounds like an excellent idea. I'll give Jill a call and let her know I'm willing to give it a go."

Westley stared at the tape in his hands. It was the video of the show where his brother had died. His mother had given it to him before she had passed, making him promise to watch it. He didn't understand why she would want him to relive the horror of his brother's death, but he had promised her. After a trying couple weeks with Emmy doing her damn hardest to avoid him and refuse to talk about things, Westley found himself staring into the dark way past midnight only too often.

Maybe, if he could lay his demons to rest, he would be better able to help her with her own. He didn't know if it would make any difference, but he felt it was worth a try. Taking a deep breath, Westley inserted the tape into the machine connected to the television. He sat in silence as the video played out. When the video got to his brother's ride, he nearly stopped it. Just seeing Joseph on that horse for the last time again made him want to die.

He gritted his teeth, forcing himself to try to discover what his mother's reason had been for wanting him to watch this horrible tape. Prior to that last jump, they had been a pair to behold. Each jump was timeless, perfect.

Like a choreographed dance the two flowed as one. Then that last jump. Westley gritted his way through it. Stopping the tape, he lay his face in his hands, sobbing. Looking back at the screen several minutes later, Westley began rewinding to the jump before that last.

As he watched again, unsure why he was forcing himself to go through it again, Westley caught a slight hesitation in the horse several strides before the last jump. He watched his brother urge the horse to keep stride, and when he tried to refuse, he had used the crop. The horse had given into his riders orders, but just as he began the descent from the ground, Westley caught sight of something he hadn't seen the last time.

The bit in the horse's mouth was skewered, off, Westley stared. Trying to pinpoint what was off about it. The horse refused to make the jump, stiffening his front legs inches away from the ground line, and sinking his haunches down as he slammed to a stop. His brother's form was already too far forward, Westley rubbed his face. His brother had lost his center long before the stallion refused the jump, and Westley watched as he flew through the air.

The moment Westley realized his brother would have been thrown into the air no matter if the horse had refused or not hit him like a stone to the head. He could see it now, as he slowed the film down, the part he had not seen from the bleachers, or even after as he tried to make it to the paramedics. In the video, he could see the broken headstall hanging from the horse as he came to a halt, painfully pulling on his sensitive mouth.

Westley thought he had received the only shock he would for the night, but as the video continued to play, he watched the then five-year-old horse as he paced on the opposite side of the jump from his now dead rider. The horse was frantic, pawing the ground, thrashing his head, and running the length of the jump. Even more astonishing was the moment the horse bolted toward the jump, determined to find his rider. Westley watched as the horse vaulted over the jump with no rider. He had not been aware of any of this while he fought the crowds to get to his brother.

The horse had made the jump but got caught up in his reins on the landing, causing himself to trip. Thrashing, the horse fought off the people trying to help him as he tried in desperation to reach his rider. The last image was that of the blood red horse lowering his head to nudge the man lying upon the ground, broken and dead.

Westley felt the sob that tore from his chest like a lightning bolt to the heart. He had been wrong. So wrong. All of these years he had blamed the horse he had loved so dearly when it had never been the horse's fault. The horse had not blatantly ignored his rider and refused the jump. He had tried to tell his rider something was wrong, but Joseph had been too intent on the jump, too intent on winning. He had refused to heed the horse's warnings and forced the animal's hand.

Had Joseph not been so off center when the horse refused, he probably would have fallen in front of the horse with minimal injuries. Rewinding the video to the stride after the jump prior to the final jump, Westley watched intently. He saw it. Only moments after the landing, there was a subtle jerk in the horses head, the moment when the leather headstall had snapped. It was followed by the brief hesitation from the horse and the moment when Joseph had lost sight of his training and forced the horse forward. Westley knew, if Fever had taken that jump at that moment, he would probably be dead with Joseph.

Long minutes passed as Westley stared out the dark window of his room. For five years he had hated that horse fiercely. He had laid part of the blame on the horse, and the rest on himself, telling himself he should have trained him better, should have refused to let Joseph ride the horse, when all this time, the horse had tried to warn him.

Tears streaked his face, and Westley didn't care. He had been so wrong. How could he be so blind? Standing, Westley walked out of his room, across the house, and sprinted off the porch. Stopping in front of Fever's stall, Westley stared at the stout horse who nickered hello. Taking a few tentative steps forward, Westley wrapped his arms around the stallion's neck, laying his face in the long mane, and sobbed.

"I'm so sorry, Fuil Fiabhras. I let you down. I was so ready to place blame, I didn't stop to think about what a good man you were. God, forgive me, Joseph."

Emmy walked slowly out onto the porch. She had been in the kitchen when Westley streaked past her. At first, she feared something was wrong, but as she stepped onto the porch, she could see the silhouette of the man embracing the horse. Sucking in a breath, Emmy watched the scene as tears fell from her own eyes. She didn't know what had happened to bridge the gap between Westley and his horse, but she was infinitely grateful it had finally happened.

Emmy turned, heading back into the house, back to her lonely room, and her lonely bed. When she got there, Emmy pulled the worn out pink stuffed horse toy from beneath her blanket and hugged it close to her chest. Inhaling as she curled up on the bed with the stuffed animal, she thought that if she tried hard enough, she could still smell the flowery scent of her sweet little Grace.

As her lids drifted close, she whispered, "I love you little Grace."

-10-

Emmy's body hurt. She was completely worn out. She had competed in three very difficult and trying shows in a two-week period, and she was beginning to feel the toll of having to be the only experienced rider showing for Lost Acres. She was really looking forward to the day Pam came back to riding full-time, but she also understood that it would take time for Pam's body to heal.

The summer was fading in the South, and all around her, Emmy could see the signs. The leaves had lost their lush green vibrancy and began fading toward yellow. The fall was one of Emmy's favorite seasons, and she looked forward to the cooler days. The evenings were already getting dark earlier, and the night now brought with it a slight chill. Watching Wind play with the jolly ball Emmy had given him, Emmy sighed.

She knew she would not be going to any Finals this year. Her trainees were all still too young and too novice. Although Olympic Thunder was performing great in the shows so far, Emmy would not push any youngster too hard too fast. She had seen too many times the devastating consequences that could happen for horse and rider.

Ru and Shamrock were making great strides toward the winner's circle as well. This past weekend Emmy had entered Ru into her first show jumping course, and although she'd had to work hard to keep the mare controlled, she had done incredibly well and had taken third. For a headstrong five-year-old's first time in the jumping course that was a great place to be. Shamrock excelled in dressage and was slowly improving his jumping form.

Michelle had been a godsend. The eighteen year arrived promptly at six fifty every morning and worked her tail off. She had been showing several of the intermediate horses for Emmy at the events, which removed a huge load off of Emmy's shoulders. The young woman had great form, a great attitude, and overall a sweet personality. Emmy had begun working with her on the horses she showed, helping her to advance her riding even further.

Rubbing her chin, Emmy realized what the beginning of fall meant. Michelle would be attending college full-time soon, and Emmy would have to work around her schedule. She was proud of the young woman for making the choice to attend school, so she would do whatever she had to do to work with her schedule.

Unfortunately, that meant she would have to put out some new want ads. She needed more help. They were just too busy for her to handle all her lessons, showing, and training the young horses both her own and the ones who had been sent to her. As she thought over all of this, Westley appeared at her side.

"You seem like you have a lot on your mind today, Emmy. Is everything all right? You did great at the show this weekend, by the way."

Emmy smiled but didn't remove her gaze from the dark horse romping before her.

"Thanks, Westley. I'm all right, just thinking is all. Michelle's going to be starting school soon, and well, with the amount of horses here who need training and showing, I just feel like I've run myself a little thin."

Westley studied her profile. "I agree, Emmy. You've got too much on your plate right now for just one experienced trainer."

Shaking her head, Emmy sighed. "Well, I have to pay the bills, I have loans I need to repay, and horses to feed, trucks to maintain, and the list goes on and on."

"Well, what are you thinking? Are you going to hire another trainer? That can get tricky you know, having to share your place with someone else, maybe they'll have a different way of doing things."

Emmy glanced at him then. "Yep. I know, I have thought about all of that, but in the long run, even if I hire an army to do all the minor things around here, I'm still only one person."

Westley regarded Emmy for a few minutes. He had thought about offering to step up into the role of trainer, even thought about showing again, now that he felt some of the guilt over his brother's death slipping away, but every time he tried, the words stuck on his tongue.

"Well, I guess if that's your only option, I'm sure it wouldn't be too hard to find a trainer willing to come on and work here."

Frowning, Emmy felt her ire rising. "Why can't you do it, Westley? I have ridden that horse, I have seen what you are capable, both as a trainer and as a rider, but still, you refuse. Why? Should I worry that your stay here won't be very long-lived? Is that it?"

Westley stared at Emmy, frowning at the frustration he could hear in her voice.

"I never said I wanted to train Emmy, and I made my stance on showing clear from day one. Why are you getting upset with me?"

Emmy threw her hands up in the air. Walking towards the house, she wanted to scream at him. She wanted to ask why he had not tried to win her over more, why he hadn't touched her, kissed her. Was it all just a game for him?

"It doesn't matter Westley. I know what you said, and I can see that your investment here is not for the long haul. Just forget I brought it up at all."

Westley stared at her retreating back. Walking forward briskly, Westley grabbed her by the shoulder, pulling her back around to face him. "What is this really about Emmy?"

Staring, Emmy lifted her chin in defiance. "Let me go, Westley. You don't want to be here, to deal with what you feel for a messed up woman. I can't say I blame you. Maybe it's just time we both forget this and move on."

Westley stared at her. "So this is about us, or what little us there is? What do you want me to do Emmy? You avoid me like the plague. When we have been alone together, things have been…"

"Disastrous?" Emmy felt the emotions rise up within her. She was tired of being afraid, tired of waiting to see if Westley would try to win her over again.

Running his fingers through his hair in his trade-mark move, Westley groaned. "I wasn't going to say disastrous Emmy, it's just that, when we are together, and something happens, you always freak out, and I have been trying, but I honestly don't know what move is right anymore. If I push too hard, you shut down, get afraid. If I leave you alone, you get upset."

"Well, you have known that I am a screwed-up mess since the beginning. I didn't ask you to come on to me Westley. I didn't ask you to kiss me. I never wanted to feel this way for a man when I don't even know how to be with a man."

"Maybe if you would try to let go of all the hurt and fear, maybe then you could have a real relationship with me, but sometimes, I feel like you don't want to let go of what happened. You just want to hold on and keep everyone else out!"

Emmy's face showed her shock and hurt at his words. Westley regretted them immediately. The truth was, he was drowning. He didn't know how to help her, and he didn't know how to be here with her and yet have to keep such a distance.

"You are one to talk about wallowing in the past Westley. You keep me out just as much as I do. I think it would be best if you left. This thing between us, whatever it was, it's never going to work."

Westley's face drained of its color. He hadn't seen this coming. "Emmy, you cannot be serious…"

Emmy stalked away. "You're never going to get what you want here with me Westley. You don't even trust me with your own secrets."

Westley called her name several times. She refused to respond. Standing there, with the southern wind whipping his shirt and hair around him, Westley felt lost. What should he do? On the one hand, he wanted Emmy, wanted her like no other, but on the other hand, he was frustrated. Emotionally and sexually frustrated. He had to fight every day to keep his control around her, to walk a fine line not to push her too far. Maybe she was right, maybe it was never going to work. Westley kicked the fence. Why? What the hell kind of man was he? He couldn't be what Emmy needed. He saw that now.

Greg watched in alarm as Westley toted his stuff out to his truck. He had no idea what had happened, but when Emmy had stormed into the house, slamming the screen and trying to hide her tears from him as she had fled upstairs, Greg's heart had dropped. Seeing Westley's stony face told him something had happened between them, and it wasn't good.

"Westley, what happened? Why are you packing your stuff? You can't leave. Emmy needs you, you know that."

Turning toward the boy he had grown attached to, Westley sighed. "She doesn't need me Greg. I don't know what she needs. A better man than me, I guess."

Greg shook his head. This was not good, not good at all. He had seen a different side to Emmy ever since this man had come here, and he had a really bad feeling about Westley leaving.

"Please, Westley, whatever happened, I'm sure you guys can work it out."

Westley got into his truck and slammed the door. Turning to the distraught teen, he sighed.

"Tell Emmy I will send someone for the horses as soon as I get things figured out. Take care of yourself, Gregory."

Emmy watched Westley's truck pull down the long driveway. Her heart felt like it was breaking all over again. He may have only been here for a few short months, but the man had managed to find a place within Emmy's heart. A place she had thought broken beyond repair. Westley had shown her what it meant to feel emotionally and physically attracted to a man, but now, she realized that she was just too broken to ever have a life with anyone else.

She admitted that it was her own fault he left. She had, after all, told him to leave, she just never thought that he would actually leave without trying. She hadn't thought Westley was a quitter, but now, watching the Chevy fade into the distance, she realized maybe she just wasn't enough for him to fight for. Her issues were too many, and fear was not easy to overcome.

Sighing Emmy looked at herself in the mirror. What she saw was not a beautiful woman. What she saw still was a sixteen-year-old girl who had just gone through hell and wore the hollow eyes of one whose soul was fractured. Looking away, Emmy felt the onslaught of tears overcome her again. Crawling into bed, she grabbed the pink horse and fell asleep with the claws of depression sinking into her.

Pam listened to Greg on the other end of the line. She could tell the boy was distraught. What he told her caused Pam's heart to stutter. Hanging up the receiver, she balanced the dark-haired infant on her hip as she turned to her husband.

"Emmy's in trouble. I need to go over there. Do you want to come, or stay here with the baby? I don't know how long it'll be."

David, frowning, glanced up in concern. "What's going on? Has she been hurt? I think I better go with you."

"Fine, let's go. I'll fill you in on the drive, but apparently, Westley left, and Emmy's in really bad shape."

Firing up the dodge, David frowned. He had not seen this coming. Westley had seemed to be truly dedicated to Emmy. "What do you mean he left? Did something happen?"

Along the drive, Pam told David what Emmy had told her a few weeks back, and then she relayed Greg's story, telling him how apparently Emmy hadn't left her room for nearly a week. Greg had been forced to call and cancel all of her lessons for her.

"Surely she has come down to eat, or go out to the stables. That doesn't seem like Emmy at all. She's been through hell, I can't see her breaking now over a guy she hardly knew."

Pam stared at her husband. She really loved him, and he was a brilliant man, but sometimes, he could be daft as hell. "David, don't you see? She was in love with him."

Emmy groaned at the throbbing in her head. It seemed to have begun pounding even louder than before. Rubbing her temples, she sighed. A voice penetrated through the fog of her mind.

"Emmy Everhart, if you don't open this door right this second David is going to break it down! I am not joking with you, young lady!"

Emmy frowned. Why was Pam here? She wasn't supposed to come for another day at least. Moving her weak, tired muscles, Emmy wobbled toward the door. Opening it, she was blasted immediately by the force of her stubborn friend.

"Emmy! You smell terrible. You look terrible, you must have lost ten pounds! Geez! Pull yourself together woman. You have a stable to run, a boy to take care of, and horses waiting for you, and that's not even to mention the Grand Prix Finals to attend. I don't give a rat's ass what happened with Westley, but I'll be damned if I'm going to watch you wither away in depression!"

Pam stormed past her, leaving Emmy to peer up at the sheepish and concerned faces of David and Greg. The boy had a guilty expression as he stepped forward.

"I'm sorry Emmy, but I had to call her. I was worried sick about you all week. I didn't know what else to do."

Emmy stared at Greg. "It's been a whole week? That cannot be right. I just laid down last night when Westley left…"

From behind her in the bathroom, Pam bellowed. "It's been a goddamned week, Emmy, now get your sorry hide in this shower!"

Emmy winced. Greg smiled apologetically, and David grinned at the expression on Emmy's face. He was reminded of one of the many reasons he loved the dark-haired beauty. Right now, however, he wanted to hunt Westley down and kick his ass all the way back to Ireland.

Emmy approached the dark-haired firing squad with trepidation. Pam wasted no time stripping the wrinkled nightgown off of her friend.

"Now, take a shower, and then you can tell me what happened, ok. I'm going to get you some tea. Don't try anything stupid, all right."

Seated in the patio chair with a thick soft robe wrapped around herself, Emmy shivered. She couldn't seem to get warm even though the temperature was still in the eighties. Behind her, Pam ran the brush lovingly through her long thick deep red waves.

"You ready to tell me what happened between you two that caused him to leave? He didn't seem like the kind of guy to give up so easily."

Sipping the warm jasmine tea, Emmy sighed. She needed to face the facts. "He left because I told him to."

When Pam's jaw dropped, Emmy told her everything, from their first kiss to their fallouts, to the time at the dinner party. She told her about Westley crying against his horse in the middle of the night, and about their argument that ultimately led to his leaving.

Pam was silent for several moments, absorbing all of the information thrown at her.

"Wow, Emmy. I can understand your fear and frustration, but I guess I can see how he would feel lost as to how to treat you too. I am curious what was in his past, but honestly, I still cannot believe he just left. I thought surely he was the one to show you what love really meant. Sometimes, it's not pretty, nor easy, but when you want someone that much, you persevere. You don't run away at the smallest hurdles."

Emmy stared into the fields.

"Pam, you know I'm not going to the Grand Prix this year, right? None of my horses are ready, and although Mr. Geraldo has several great jumpers, they are not Grand Prix material. The one he has that may come close is only a three-year-old, and Wind is nowhere near ready to be ridden, let alone taken to such a large-scale show."

Pam bit her lip. "You are going to the show. And so am I. And, we'll be entering Michelle into the lower level events. Lost Acres needs the publicity. You need the therapy. The only thing that ever brings you out of your depression is these horses. Forget about Westley. If it was meant to be, it will, and if not, then he was just a hurdle along the way."

Emmy studied her friend. She had the terrible feeling plans were hatching inside the terrifying mind of her friend. She didn't know what Pam was thinking, but she knew there was no point arguing with her. Watching the mist rise over the fields and shroud the grazing horses in its shadow, Emmy sighed. She knew Pam was right. This place, these animals, they had always been the way she healed.

Westley picked up the phone. Watching the planes taking off in the distance, he debated entering the airport. He had been lost ever since leaving Emmy. He had no direction in life anymore. He didn't know whether to stay here or go home to Ireland.

"Yeah, this is Westley Galway."

"Westley. It's Pamela Ryans."

Westley's heart stopped. "Pam. Is Emmy all right? Has something happened? God, tell me she's all right."

Pam was quite a moment. "Well, at least I know you still care. Emmy's fine…well, she's ok. Anyway, she doesn't know I'm calling you."

Westley released his breath. "All right. I'm glad she is ok. What can I do for you Mrs. Ryans?"

"I want to make a deal with you, Westley. I don't want you to take your horses from Lost Acres."

Westley frowned. His curiosity was definitely piqued.

"Well, that's interesting. Why would you want me to leave them there when Emmy told me to leave?"

"Look, Westley, I don't know why you left. I know what she said, but sometimes we women get scared or upset and we say things we don't always mean. I want you to leave the horses there, and I want you to let her ride one of those stallions. She needs a horse good enough to go to the Finals. You don't show them or breed them. They are wasting away and they should be shown for the amazing animals they are."

Westley considered her words. Before he could form an answer, the woman continued.

"There is another reason. If the horses are there, and one day you find yourself wishing you had tried harder with Emmy, you'll have the excuse to come back. You don't have to pay anything. We will cover the cost of keeping them for the chance to show them."

Westley sunk back into his seat. Looking out the front windshield of his truck as another plane flew off into the distance, Westley pondered the woman's words.

"All right. I agree. You can show the stallions. I'll give you until after the Finals. If neither Emmy nor I have changed our minds, then I'm taking them."

Hanging up the receiver, Westley stared into the foggy morning. His jaw ticked. Who was he kidding? He would never change his mind about Emmy, but he also felt it was never going to work. He may as well move on with his life. He felt this hurdle was just too big for either of them to clear.

∞∞∞∞

-11-

Emmy stared at Pam in disbelief. "You did what Pamela Ryans?" She could not believe her friend. She had forgiven her for going behind her back and making a deal with Westley, but this, Emmy didn't know how to react to.

Beside her, David sent her a sympathetic look. "I tried to talk her out of it, love, really, but she would not be swayed on this."

Emmy groaned. Watching the baby trying to chew his chubby fists, Emmy felt herself soften. How could she be upset with the person who cared for her more than anyone else in her life? Taking the baby from David, she cooed at the dark-eyed baby.

"Fine, Pam. I will do it, and try to get through it with minimal breakdowns, but you owe me big time."

Pam tilted her head. Regarding her friend, she smiled. Emmy looked so good holding a baby. She sent up a prayer that one day Emmy would have a second chance at being a mother.

"Actually Emmy, after watching you ride Darkness today, I would say I don't owe you anything. You're going to win the Grand Prix. I think you owe me. Although, I still think the red one is the really impressive horse."

Emmy shook her head. They had been over this argument too many times. Fever was Westley's horse. He may respond well to Emmy, but in truth, he belonged to the man, and he would never perform for anyone the way he would for Westley. Emmy felt too emotional when she rode the blood red stallion. She and Darkness had developed a great bond, and she knew the stallion was the one to ride this year, at least until Wind was ready.

Pacing the porch, Emmy felt like she were about to have a nervous breakdown. She didn't know if she could do this. Her hands were clammy, and her heart raced. Maybe she wasn't ready for this. The sound of the screen door closing nearly made her jump out of her skin.

"Geez Emmy, you're as jumpy as a fresh colt on race day. Calm down. Look, why don't you go upstairs and get ready, and I'll keep an eye on the kitchen."

Pam laughed. "Although, I'm not sure my skills will be anything next to that boy's. He's a genius."

Emmy laughed, but she realized how nervous it sounded. "Yeah, he studies a lot of cooking techniques. I'm going to take you up on that. I really do need to get ready."

As Emmy stepped past Pam, her friend reached out, grabbing her hand. Holding eye contact, Pam smiled. "It will be all right, Emmy. It's time to let yourself heal, ok."

Emmy swallowed and nodded emotionally. She really didn't know if she was ready, but she had been doing a lot of thinking since Westley left, and she believed that healing was exactly what needed to happen before she could have a real relationship.

Coming down the stairs, Emmy was all nerves. Straightening the long blue dress she had chosen to wear, Emmy checked the French braid in her hair again. She was a mess of nerves. She knew this was something she needed to do, but that didn't make facing it any easier. As she neared the bottom of the wide staircase, Emmy could hear the sound of many voices downstairs.

She realized that this was the most people that she'd had in her house, and for a brief moment, the sound washed away her nerves. The sound of children's laughter greeted her ears, and Emmy swallowed the overpowering emotions. A small smile graced her lips as Emmy realized this was something she had always hoped for. The sound of children and family in her home.

Pam had given her a shock when she had informed her that she had invited all of Emmy's family here for Thanksgiving, along with the Fitzgerald's, and Westley. Emmy didn't know which one frightened her more. The prospect of having her family here with her wounds still so raw was overwhelming, but the thought of seeing Westley again was what truly had her heart racing.

At the bottom of the landing, Emmy found herself face to face with Ian. He had stood there waiting for her. His face had healed, all except the pink scar that now ran across one cheek. He no longer had any casts, although Emmy noticed he leaned on a cane. The expression on his face nearly brought tears to Emmy's eyes.

"Emmy, I cannot tell you how much it means to me, to all of us that you have welcomed us to your home. I want my little sister back, and I pray that one day, you'll forgive me."

Emmy bit her lip. She didn't want to cry so early in the evening. Not trusting her voice, she gave her brother a nod. Stepping forward, she allowed him to pull her into a gentle hug. It required just about everything to keep from breaking down in his arms. Stepping away, Emmy saw Miranda approaching.

"Emmy, you look amazing. I wish I could have a figure like you still do." Miranda's soft hazel eyes shone with tears.

Emmy studied her sister-in-law in her dark purple dress. She was still beautiful, with her abundantly curly strawberry blond hair, and creamy complexion. Her body had gained soft curves, the kind motherhood brings, but to Emmy, the woman was still stunning.

"Miranda, you are still so beautiful. Having a couple kids and still looking the way you do is a feat in itself."

Laughing, Miranda pulled two children forward. The boy, who looked around eleven or twelve, was the spitting image of his father. "This is Luke."

Turning to face his son, he said, "Luke, this is your Aunt Emmy."

The boy said a bashful hello. Emmy smiled at him. Then, she felt the tug on her hand and glanced down. The little four-year-old toddler looked up at Emmy with big golden eyes. Her hair was a shade darker red than her mother's, but with the same ringlet curls covering her head. She smiled at Emmy as she pointed to the house.

"Play with puppy?" Emmy followed the girl's finger to see a patient Feather wagging her tail in the corner. Emmy smiled.

"Yes, you can play with Feather. She's just a puppy still." Emmy and Miranda exchanged smiles as the little girl squealed and headed for the object of her attention.

"That was Ellen. She is very fond of puppies."

Emmy smiled. "You have beautiful children. I am very happy for the two of you, and your family."

Emmy removed her gaze from Miranda's as she noticed the sadness creep in. She knew what the cause was, but she refused to go there tonight. She had made the decision that tonight was about reconnecting and forgiving family. Not about getting caught up in the past.

Hearing a commotion from the kitchen, Emmy excused herself to check things out. Just as she neared the entrance to the kitchen, two dark-haired boys came squealing and bounding out, cookies shoved into each hand, and one in their mouth as they ran off. Behind them, Vadetta wielded the rolling pin.

"You two little monsters better not try that again! You'll spoil your dinner! Don't make me call your father."

Emmy tried to keep her laughter at bay. The picture of her mother chasing her grandsons from the kitchen with a rolling pin brought a flood of heart-wrenching memories to mind. When her mother looked up and saw her, she froze. Lowering the rolling pin, she smiled sheepishly.

"Why, Emmy. You look absolutely stunning. Your home here is lovely. It's so big and beautiful and the gardens…" she trailed off, and Emmy could tell she was unsure of how to act with her.

"Thank you. It's taken a lot of work. I'm guessing those little heathens were Aaron's boys? I can still picture you chasing him out of the kitchen just that way."

Vadetta's eyes softened. She seemed about to say something when a dark-haired woman approached them. Emmy had never seen the woman before. Her skin was exceptionally pale, and her hair and eyes very dark. There was something foreign, exotic about her, but Emmy couldn't place it.

Vadetta noticed the woman and smiled. "Ah, yes. Emmy, this is Letitia, Aaron's wife. Letitia, this is Emmy."

The woman smiled with politeness. "Emmy, it is a pleasure to finally meet you. Thank you so much for inviting us to your lovely home. How you take care of all this, I cannot imagine."

Emmy smiled. "It certainly keeps me busy." As Emmy watched the woman excuse herself saying she needed to check on her monstrous sons, Vadetta turned to Emmy.

"She's from France. Aaron met her there during a college trip to Europe. She's a sweet woman, she came home with him, and you can imagine my surprise."

Emmy nodded. "Do they only have the two boys?"

"Oh, goodness no. They have two girls as well. The boys are twins; they are ten, Dillon and Daniel. The girls, Valerie and Chloe are six and two. They are all good kids, just the boys are very rambunctious."

Emmy laughed. She hadn't realized Aaron had so many. It made her feel old and even lonelier. Here she was still unmarried and without a child to hold, while her siblings had blossoming families. Hearing the sound of a man clearing his throat behind her, Emmy turned to find Connor and a voluptuous blond standing with several children.

"Emmy, I would like to introduce you to my family. This is my wife, Arleta, and our daughters. Samantha, Erika, and Blanche."

Emmy studied the woman with her short blond hair, and curvy bust and hips. Her big blue eyes and heart shaped face made her very beautiful. The three girls all followed after their mother, with their golden blond locks and bright blue eyes. They looked to range in age from nine to three. Emmy smiled.

"Wow, Connor. Three girls. I surely hope you have more than one bathroom at your house." When they all laughed, Emmy sobered. "Arleta, it is a pleasure to meet you. Your girls are beautiful, and very lucky to gain their looks from you."

Emmy watched the woman blush, and when Connor looked at his wife, it was clear to Emmy that he loved his wife. When he looked back at her, Emmy could read the regret in his eyes. Emmy touched his shoulder when he opened his mouth to speak.

"Tonight Conner, let's not talk about the past. I am looking forward to learning what my family has been up to, and getting to know all of my adorable nieces and nephews."

Conner nodded, understanding Emmy's need not to speak about the events of the past. Emmy let out a breath as she moved into the kitchen to find Greg and Pam busy with the preparations. Pam looked up and winked.

"Connor's wife brought this amazing fruitcake, and Aaron's brought this vegetable dish that smells like heaven. Your mom brought apple-pie, pecan pie, and custard something or another." Laughing, Pam rubbed her stomach. "Miranda brought maple covered figs, brown sugar and honey ribs, and collard greens. Rae brought corned beef and cabbage, and something I can't remember the name. I think I'm going to die and go to heaven!!"

Emmy studied the beaming face of her friend. They had been best friends since their childhood. There was little Emmy didn't know about Pam, and right then, Emmy smiled knowingly. She wondered if her friend even realized.

"Do you think David's still going to let you compete at the Finals next month when he realizes you're going to be a mommy again, Pam?"

The dark-haired beauty froze. With a startled look on her face, she shook her head, looking up at Emmy. "Emmy. I'm not…" frowning, she thought back over the past month.

"Come to think of it, I can't remember having my period, but surely it's too soon to have become pregnant again…"

Emmy laughed. "Better make an appointment with your doctor on Monday Pammy, just to be sure. You have pregnant written all over you."

Greg wrinkled his nose. "If the two of you don't mind… I am trying to cook a Thanksgiving feast here."

Laughing, the two women headed out of the kitchen to check on their guests. Emmy glanced at Pam and lowered her voice. "Has there been any word from, well, you know."

Pam sighed. She had hoped to have more time to break the news to her friend. "I'm sorry, babe. He called earlier and thanked us for the invitation, but he's gone home to Ireland for the holidays."

Emmy felt her heart sink. She hadn't realized how much she had been wanting to see Westley. "Ok." When she turned away, Emmy tried to erase the disappointment from her mind. She had a lot to celebrate tonight. She wouldn't let the sadness of not seeing Westley cloud her mind.

Sitting at the long dining table, Emmy looked around herself. She felt the truth and importance of the moment wash over her. She had been terrified at the prospect of having to face her family tonight, but here she sat, her heart swelling with love for the children who laughed and played. It swelled with sadness that she had lost so many years with these kids and with each of her brothers.

Looking down the table toward the silvery hair of her mother, Emmy sighed. Her mother had aged a lot in the last decade, and though the woman was still beautiful in her regal way, the stress of the past few years certainly showed in her face. Emmy knew that her mom yearned to have her back in her life and that tonight was a huge stepping stone for all of them. Her brothers treated her with respect, and regret.

Emmy decided, sitting there at the table with this large gathering of people, that she didn't want any regrets, not in herself, nor in them. Standing, she raised her glass of champagne and cleared her throat. When all eyes had gathered on her, and the room fell silent, Emmy scanned the group, gathering her courage.

"I want to thank each of you for coming tonight, for blessing my home with the smiling faces of your children, and my table with the delicious aromas of food. I want to thank Greg and Pam for an amazing meal. I want to thank Rae and Michael, for giving me the chance to know their one-of-a-kind son. Pam and David, you two have made all of my dreams come true, and for that, I owe you the biggest thank you."

Studying her mother, and her brothers, Emmy continued, "Our road to this point has not been an easy one, and I am probably the most to blame. I held onto the past, onto my pain and anger. When some of you reached out to me, I was not ready to forgive. Tonight, being with you all, I see what I have missed out on in my bitterness. I have missed out on a family. Tonight, I realize everyone makes mistakes, and I don't want to live in their shadow anymore. I hope that we can all move on together and be a family again."

Vadetta burst into tears. Connor, his face showing Emmy his gratitude, pulled their mother into his arms. Ian, seated beside her, pulled her into a warm embrace. Aaron made eye contact with her and mouthed thank you. Emmy herself could feel the threat of tears, so she sat back down and sipped her wine. Tonight, she felt like she had crossed one of the biggest hurdles in her life.

December came in with a flourish of fresh snow and new friends. Emmy had hired two of the kids she had met through the youth program that brought troubled teens out to the ranch twice a week. The boy and girl had both been close to turning eighteen when they first began the program, and within weeks of coming to Lost Acres, it was clear to Emmy the pair of them were hardworking and bright. They had been dealt hard hands in life, and all they wanted was the chance to make something of themselves.

The boy, Johnny, was from a family who had too many children, and never enough money. He struggled to work through high school to help his parents pay the bills.

Emmy could see he was a good kid with a big heart. Hiring him to work on the ranch, she paid him more than he had made at most of his jobs and kept him out of trouble.

The girl, Abigail, had grown up in foster care, and her hopes of getting adopted had never come through. She was incredibly bright, and kind and Emmy had liked her immediately. Emmy had seen the girl's interest in the horses, and as part of her pay, she gave her riding lessons twice a week. The pair of them were a big help on the farm.

The trainer she had hired, however, was another story entirely. The man was obnoxious, stingy, and conceded. He may have come with excellent experience, and recommendations, but after only a month, he was grating on Emmy's nerves. He consistently slacked off, showed up late, and flirted with her to no end.

The man refused to clean stalls, saying it was demeaning, and to be honest, Emmy really didn't like his riding style. She hadn't even asked him to ride or train any of her horses or students. The man paid to keep his horses in the stables and train his students there. The income helped, but Emmy was close to sending him packing.

Hearing his voice, Emmy hurried into the trailer with her saddle. She needed to get things packed and get on the road to the Finals. She did not have time for any of his drama.

"Emmy, I say, Emmy? I need to speak with you. Honestly, can't you hear me? I need to know who will be here at the farm for the next week while you're at the show."

Turning, Emmy frowned at the tall blond man. "Jean-Paul. We have been over this already. Michael Fitzgerald and his wife will be staying at the house while I'm gone. Greg is going with me, as is Pam and her husband. Michelle is also going with me. There will be no youth classes or lessons this week. Johnny and Abigail will be here every day to muck stalls, feed and turn out. You don't even need to show up this week if you don't want to."

Jean-Paul looked affronted. "Why ever would you say such a thing, Emmy? I still have my lessons to attend to, after all. We cannot all go traipsing off to shows every weekend."

Rolling her eyes as she turned her back on the annoyingly needy man, Emmy tried to focus on arranging her trailer.

"Will you at least have lunch with me before you take off, Emmy? I won't get to see you for an entire week!"

Emmy rubbed her temples. "Jean-Paul, we have been over this as well, we will not be having lunch, or dinner, or any sort of thing. I have explained I am not interested in you that way. Now, please, I need to get ready."

Jean-Paul stomped away in disappointment. Emmy breathed in the cold air, relieved the man had finally gone. She had enough on her mind with the upcoming show. She had a full show schedule, a list of young inexperienced horses to load, and a pregnant Pam to worry about.

Michelle approached Emmy with the last of the tack that needed loading. "That's the rest of it, Emmy. You want me to start grabbing horses, I just saw the Ryans' pull up."

Emmy nodded. "Yeah, we need to head out. Stallions first, all right. We'll put Oly in, then Sham, followed by Maverick, and Darkness. Next, you can load Geraldo's two geldings. Scotch and Ru, we'll put with the two mares that belong to Geraldo in Pam's trailer."

Michelle nodded. "Right, got it, boss. I'll go start prepping them and bring them out as I get ready. Shipping boots and sheets for all of them, right?" At Emmy's nod, she gave her a thumbs up before running off.

When Pam walked up, they had just loaded the final horse into Emmy's trailer. She shivered, wrapping her coat around herself tightly. "Good thing there is no forecast for storms this week. Still, don't know why they hold the Finals in the middle of the blasted winter!"

Emmy laughed. "So, you sure you're up for this Pammy? David's okay with you riding in this show?"

Pam swooshed her boot in the snow. "David's all right with me riding Maverick in the dressage courses. He's not so fond of me jumping."

Emmy walked with her friend as they met Michelle with the next horse. Emmy led the mare into the trailer, grateful that all the horses they were taking loaded well.

Hoping back out, she asked, "And you, Pam? How do you feel about it?"

Pam sighed. "I don't really know Emmy. I rode through my first months with Topher. I don't want to take a chance with anything happening with the baby, but this is who I am and what I do."

Emmy thought for a moment. "I have an idea. Why don't you ride Maverick in the dressage classes you planned on doing? You know him, and he knows you. You've been competing on that horse for ten years. I will take your place on Scotch. She's still young, and if something were to go wrong, I'd never be able to forgive myself."

Pam's face brightened up. "Really? Are you sure, Emmy? That won't be too much for you? I think it would make me feel much more comfortable just to ride Mav."

Emmy nodded. Taking the lead of the gelding Michelle handed her, she smiled. "It's a plan then."

Taking a deep breath, Emmy rechecked that all the horses were settled into their stalls at the show grounds. The place was packed. People and horses came and went from every direction. She had read the names posted on the event list. The competition was steep. Even steeper than it had been the year she had won the Grand Prix on

Viewfinder. Thinking of her beloved horse, Emmy released a long sigh.

"Are you wishing you had brought Viewfinder?" When Emmy opened her eyes to see Greg watching her, Emmy nodded.

"Yeah. I am. The longer you ride a horse, the stronger the connection becomes. You can see it in the ring. When a horse and rider are not connected enough, the communication isn't there, and it's evident. I have only been working with Darkness a few months, and although he is exceptionally well trained, it's still a new partnership. With View, he and I, it was like we became one."

Greg nodded. Studying the big dark horse, he rubbed the stallions chin. "Well, I understand that, but I've seen you two working, and he seems pretty attentive to you. I think you two will be great, Emmy."

Emmy smiled in gratitude at the teenager. "Come on, let's go check on Pam and her boys. Who knows what trouble they will get into by themselves?"

Emmy's nerves mellowed only when she was on top of a horse. It was ironic because she knew for most people it was the opposite, but her soul only seemed at peace when on a horse. She had seen her mother and brothers in the stands with David and Pam, and it touched her heart that although their new relationship was insecure, they had come out to show their support.

With the taut muscles of the big black horse beneath her, Emmy brought her focus back around. She had just entered the ring, ready to run her cross-country race, the second phase of the three-day event. The previous day, she had ridden Darkness in the dressage trials. The horse had performed with amazing talent, and Emmy had big ambitions for today's run.

Taking deep slow breaths, she ran her hand down the side of the dark stallion's neck. The announcer introduced her and her mount to the audience as Emmy and Darkness walked quietly into the ring. Emmy was not a new face here at the Grand Prix, and she smiled as applause broke out through the crowd.

Darkness twitched an ear, and Emmy felt the horse too was pleased with the sound. He truly was a show horse. Some horses seem to literally shine when in the show ring, and Darkness certainly was one of them. Gathering her thoughts together, Emmy breathed slowly and focused on the obstacles ahead. As she waited for the buzzer to sound, Emmy cleared her mind of all thoughts. Her focus was so intense, the crowd faded away from her.

Her horse's ears were perked forward as he too appeared to gather himself, readying for the race that would test their endurance, ability, and training. This was no easy event, and many people were injured in this level of cross-country. Emmy knew the drill. The horse knew the drill. The buzzer sounded, and Darkness shot forward.

Galloping their way to the first obstacle, a three-foot, nine-inch high double brush with hedges and flags on either side. Darkness cleared the jump with finesse. Emmy felt her adrenaline kicking in as they approached the end of the green where a steep down-hill step waited. Advancing forward after the series of step jumps, Emmy raced up the one-hundred yard dash uphill leading to the first water jump.

Darkness took the leap into the water with no difficulty. Emmy felt the wind whip her hair, and she remembered again why she loved this sport. The muscles of her horse were strong and the power of the stallion was undeniable. Approaching the first jump located in the water, the pair trod through the thirty foot stretch of knee deep water. The jump in the center was a triangular shaped wooden arrowhead. Leaning forward as the horse leaped over the jump, Emmy felt the power of the horse to her very core.

The final jump of the four-mile track was a Normandy bank with a nearly four-foot hump and a twelve-foot distance across the top. As the pair of them flew over the wide jump, the stallion was stretched out across the top, and Emmy felt as though they soared through the air with wings. They landed with no faults at all. Something that did not happen very often in the Eventing world.

Emmy brought her horse to a canter, riding toward the exit gate. She patted the stallion fondly on his thick corded neck. He truly was a brilliant horse. Emmy thanked her lucky stars for having the opportunity to ride such a powerful horse in the Finals. She knew without a doubt that they had a real chance at coming out in the top ten. Maybe even better.

Emmy was exhilarated. The excitement of the ride still coursed through her veins, the powerful horse beneath her buzzing with energy. Riding back toward the warm-up areas, Emmy tried not to listen. She still had the show jumping event on the following day, and she knew from experience that anything could happen. She didn't want to get her hopes up. It was a little difficult though, as she reached Pam, and was immediately overcome by the cheering group heading toward them.

Emmy had at first thought the group consisted of her family, but she soon realized it wasn't just her family. About twenty others surrounded her and her horse as she hopped off of him to begin his cool down walk. Overcome with surprise, and slightly flustered, Emmy wasn't prepared for the onslaught of questions.

"Miss. Everhart, are you open to new students? Will you be giving lessons this spring? Is this your new eventer?"

Laughing, Emmy glanced at Pam mischievously. "Any questions about our equestrian facility, training, and lessons may be directed toward Mrs. Pamela Ryans."

Still laughing as she headed toward the barn, Emmy didn't miss the death look Pam had sent her before graciously speaking to the eager crowd. Emmy truly didn't think anything could bring down the excitement she felt over today's ride.

Westley watched Emmy surrounded by her crowd of fans from the stadium. He smiled reminiscently. She had blazed through today's course like a force of nature. She had been amazing, and Westley admitted that she and Dorchadas made an excellent team. The pair responded to each other as though they had been training for years, not months. He was glad he had made the decision to allow her the use of his horses, but still piqued that she had chosen the black after her infatuation with Fever.

When Westley had heard Emmy would be riding in the Finals, he had come back to the states, again. He still didn't completely understand what it was about the woman that just one magazine article with her featured could make him fly all the way back here at the drop of a dime. He was proud of her. She had been the most beautiful poised, and confident rider out there today.

Westley quietly made his way out of the grandstands, headed toward the parking lot. He'd been having a hard time these last couple months, keeping his distance from Emmy. He had even tried dating but never made it past the first dinner. Everything about that woman had offended him. Her hair wasn't the deep mahogany red of Emmy's. Her eyes were not blue enough. She didn't know a damn thing about horses.

Westley had come to a few decisions when he had been home in Ireland with his sister's family. He wanted, needed to be around horses. It was in his blood, and in his soul. He had come a long way since realizing Joseph's death had really been an accident, the bridle had snapped, and there was really no one to hold blame for it. Now,

Westley felt he was finally ready to step back into the life he had torn himself out of.

He wanted to be a trainer. He wanted to feel the rush as he soared through the air in the shows. He wanted to pick and choose which horses would make better progeny. He wanted it all back. And, he wanted Emmy. The yearning he had felt for her the lonely winter months that he had spent in the coldness of Ireland had only driven the point home. She was the woman he wanted. She was the woman who was meant for him, and no matter the hurdles they had to cross, he was determined to be with her.

Emmy felt the tears in her eyes as she sat the golden trophy up onto the mantel beside the one she and Viewfinder had won. She hadn't been able to believe it when she had been informed she'd taken first in the Grand Prix on Darkness. She had brought home several second and thirds on Ru, Shamrock, and Thunder. All of her horses had placed in the top five, and she was incredibly grateful. Pam had placed first in her dressage classes with Maverick, and Michelle had brought home several firsts and seconds. The publicity it would bring Lost Acres alone would be worth all the hard work.

Emmy could hear the wind gaining force outside. She had not been home for more than a couple hours, but already it looked like rain in the near future. Emmy touched her fingertips to the photo of her daughter before heading outside. The wind rattled the windowpanes and whipped her coat around her. She knew it was going to be a long cold January.

∞∞∞∞

-12-

Emmy toted the wheelbarrow out of the stall; pulling her coat back on, she prepared to head into the bitterly cold morning. The sky overhead was already dark and dreary, with all indications pointing toward another rain. The snow seemed to have vanished to be replaced by the continual rainstorms that had turned the stables into a muddy mess. Maneuvering the heavy load, Emmy headed out to the manure pile.

Sighing, Emmy fought the wind as she dumped her load. Looking at the growing pile, she thought, just another thing on the constantly growing list that needs doing. Michelle had gone on vacation with her family for the month, and Greg was with his Mother and father in Scotland. That left Emmy two hands short with an already understaffed situation. Hard work had never been something Emmy shied away from. She gritted her teeth against the bitter wind and headed back into the barn.

Hearing the crunch of tires on gravel, Emmy glanced up only to roll her eyes. Jean-Paul's Mercedes pulled up, whipping rocks around. Emmy shook her head. Too many times she had asked the obnoxious man to slow down. For, Emmy, this was her last straw with the man. He hadn't bothered to show up all week or even call. Emmy had to take care of his horses as well as all the others, but what was worse was when his handful of students had shown up for their group lesson with no Jean-Paul.

Being forced to give the lesson herself, or have their center look bad for the lack of professionalism from their trainers, Emmy had been seething. The situation put her late for her own lessons and left her in a foul mood all day. When she had called Jean-Paul, confronting him about his absence, the man had sounded three sheets to the wind.

Emmy pretended not to notice when Jean-Paul sauntered into the barn. He was dressed as usual, in clothes far too expensive to be wearing around a stable. When she realized he was heading toward the stall she was in, she clamped down on her temper, preparing to deal with the annoying man.

"Emmy, darling. I am so sorry for the other day. I really appreciate you taking care of my lesson for me. I honestly don't know how I forgot about it."

Emmy glanced up. "Yeah, that's a really good question, Jean-Paul. How did you manage to forget your responsibilities here as a trainer for an entire week? Do you think horses take care of themselves?"

The blond man sent her a sardonic smile. "Emmy, I'm sure it wasn't that hard for you. After all, isn't that why you have people working here? To clean up the poop these horses produce, while we do the training?"

Emmy could feel her ire rising. "I do not hire people to clean up poop. I hire them because I cannot run this place by myself. I have absolutely no problem shoveling horse crap. You would learn well to take yourself off of that pedestal sometimes and take care of your animals yourself as well."

Laughing, Jean-Paul leaned against the wall. "Oh Emmy, that's what makes you so refreshing. You have such a sweet positive outlook on those who will never be as good as us. Really. A Grand Prix winner should not have to shovel her own horse poo."

Her jaw ticked. He was really pissing her off now. "Jean-Paul, you are an obtuse ass. Excuse me."

Turning back to her shoveling, Emmy didn't realize that Jean-Paul had entered the stall until it was too late. When she felt the leather of his gloved hands slide over her back, Emmy whirled around in anger.

"What the hell do you think you are doing? How dare you touch me in such an inappropriate way!"

Jean-Paul stepped closer to Emmy. Smiling like a serpent, he said, "Oh, Emmy. You know what you need? You need a big strong man between those lovely thighs of yours. I think a little sex would go a long way toward cooling that haughty attitude of yours."

Emmy froze. Her mind was caught somewhere between fear and anger. Jean-Paul mistook her silence and closed the gap between them. Emmy was trapped between the man and the wall. Inside, she trembled. She had been here before. Taking control of her resolve, Emmy told herself to get a grip. She would never be in that position again. Never.

"Jean-Paul, you have two minutes to get your sorry hide off my property. I want you and anything that you have brought here gone by nightfall. You just voided the contract you signed."

Laughing, the Frenchman leaned toward Emmy. "Don't be afraid, pretty girl. You'll enjoy it, I promise."

Emmy had enough. Leaning slightly toward Jean-Paul, she brought her knee up harshly between the man's legs. "Get out!"

Jean-Paul doubled over, swearing under his breath. He reached out toward Emmy in anger. Seeing the threat in his eyes, Emmy lunged past him, running from the stall. She hastened toward the house. She would not allow this man to do anything to her. She had just jumped onto the porch stairs when an intense pain hit her in the head. Crying out, Emmy reached back to feel the sticky wetness on the back of her scalp.

Beside her, a rock wobbled, stained with her blood. Looking up, she saw the furious form of Jean-Paul stalking forward toward her. Emmy sucked in a breath at the murderous look on his face. Running into the house, Emmy picked up the receiver and dialed nine-one-one. She could hear the heavy footfalls of the man as he strode up the porch. When the dispatcher answered, Emmy, told her she was being attacked.

The sound of wood splintering from the back of the house hit Emmy's ears just as she recited her address. Tears were threatening to overwhelm her. She needed to get her rifle. The woman told her to stay on the phone, but Emmy knew that wasn't possible. Dropping the phone, she ran toward the den where she kept her gun safe.

She never made it that far. Jean-Paul grabbed her by the hair, yanking her roughly backward. Emmy shrieked, feeling the pain in her already wounded head.

"You little whore. How dare you! You think you are too good for me? I tried being nice, I tried flirting, but no. Emmy Everhart is too much a prude to ever go out. You should have taken me up on my many offers, bitch. Now, we'll do it the hard way."

Emmy clenched her jaw. "You will not get anything from me. The police are on their way. They will be here before you get to do anything. You're going to jail where you can never lay a hand on another woman again."

Jean-Paul pulled Emmy toward him. With the back of his hand, he whacked her across the face, sending her flying across the room. Emmy hit the floor with a groan.

Her face felt like it was going to explode. Jean-Paul took a step toward her. Emmy heard a sound, so soft and faint she almost missed it. Her eyes snapped to the doorway, and relief spread through her chest. Rainy stood in the doorway, her head low, and lips pulled back in aggression. Her tail was high and her hackles raised along her shoulders.

The growl she had released was so low, Jean-Paul was completely oblivious to the dog. Reaching down, he grabbed Emmy, prepared to yank her off the floor. What he wasn't prepared for was the sudden impact of something leaping onto his back. Feeling the intense pain that suddenly tore through his shoulder, he dropped Emmy, spinning around with the one-hundred and twenty-pound dog locked onto his shoulder.

Emmy leaped to her feet, watching the blood that poured from the man's shoulder where Rainy had a vice grip with her teeth. The sound of sirens in the distance reached Emmy's ears, and she felt like finally, things would be all right. Jean-Paul smashed himself into the wall, causing the dog to lose her grip. Rainy jumped out in front of Emmy, her fur stained with his blood as she prepared to defend her owner.

Jean-Paul, holding his shoulder, heard the sirens as well. Glaring at Emmy, he looked around frantically. Running to the door, he turned back toward her.

"This is not over, bitch."

Emmy watched, still stunned as the man fled from the house. Walking slowly toward the door, Emmy patted the dog beside her as sobs escaped her. "That's a good girl, Rainy."

The next hour, Emmy spent with the police. They insisted she go have herself checked out at the emergency room, to assess the injury to her head and face. The police investigators were at her house, taking samples from the blood on the carpet, and documenting the broken back door. To Emmy's horror, Jean-Paul had managed to get out of her driveway before the cops had shown up. The thought that this man was still on the loose sent shivers of fear down her spine.

She didn't want to be at that house alone with a man like that on the loose, hell-bent on getting even with her. She had filed an emergency restraining order and already called Pam and David. They were dealing with the lawyer issues of the contract between them and Jean-Paul. Fortunately, he had broken the contract the second he had touched her, and then again with the damaged property. They had put a very strong sexual harassment and property damage clause in the contract originally.

Pam, of course, was freaking out. She was determined that Emmy would come stay with them that night, but Emmy couldn't do that. She had animals to take care of and to be honest, she was afraid of what the deranged man might do. One of the worse pieces of information was when the police had informed her that Jean-Paul had two other sexual harassment cases filed against him, and an assault from Florida.

Fortunately, the wound to Emmy's scalp had only required a few stitches, and there were no broken bones in her face. As grateful as she was, Emmy still felt like her face had been crushed. Her right cheek was blue and purple, and her eye was swollen. Emmy was beyond grateful for her dog. If it hadn't been for her, Emmy knew it would have ended with her in much worse condition.

Emmy was grateful to finally be home. The day had been quiet, and Jean-Paul's horses had been picked up earlier in the day by a horse transport company. Unfortunately, the Bastard was still missing, but Emmy kept a loaded handgun on her at all times. The police had units patrolling the area day and night, and there was a patrol unit monitoring who came and went from her driveway. Pam had not wanted her to go home alone, but Emmy insisted she would be ok.

Looking down at the German shepherd lovingly, Emmy scratched her ear. Double-checking all the newly installed locks on the doors and windows, Emmy headed toward the stairs. David had not given up on his worry. He'd had the door replaced, new locks put in, and the blood cleaned up from the den while Emmy stayed at their place. He had also had a state of the art alarm installed, and although Emmy appreciated their concern, she was still trying to remember how the damn thing worked.

David had assured her that any suspicious activity around the house would be reported directly to the police. Emmy had to admit, she would definitely sleep a little better now that the alarm was there. Heading upstairs with her two dogs, Emmy locked her door, checked her second story windows, and finally headed to bed. It had been a very long and trying week, and she was honestly exhausted.

The buzzing of the telephone, ringing incessantly woke Emmy early in the predawn light of the following morning. Sitting up, she rubbed her eyes. When the phone began buzzing again, Emmy sighed. Picking up, she croaked hello.

"Emmy! Geez, it took you forever to pick up. I was about to call the cops! Are you all right?"

Emmy smiled at the worry in Pam's voice. "Yes, mama Pammy. I was sound asleep, what is it anyway, like three am?"

There was a long pause. "Yeah, close to. Listen, Emmy, I have to tell you something, and you're not going to like it."

Emmy frowned. "All right Pam, I'm fully awake and listening now. What's going on?"

"They found Jean-Paul about an hour ago." Pam paused before continuing. "He and two others were hauling some horses. They found him on the road behind Lost Acres. He had ten of our horses."

Emmy felt her heart drop. Her mind reeled. "How is that possible? I didn't hear a thing last night, and Rainy and Feather didn't either. What horses Pam?"

Emmy didn't like the silence. Her heart pounded loudly in her chest as her worry began to escalate. "View? Please tell me not View."

Pam released a long breath. "Yeah, Emmy, he had Viewfinder. And Westley's two stallions, and Maverick, and some of the others. Calm down, they are all fine. The police are bringing them back right now. They said him and some guys snuck in on foot from the back pastures and led the horses out. That's probably why you didn't hear anything and the dogs didn't react. Let's just be thankful all the horses are all right, and they finally got the creep. Not only will he be facing assault, breaking and entering, and attempted rape charges, but now he's going to face theft as well."

Emmy let out a long exhale. "Thank god they are all right. I just cannot believe I slept through all of that. It makes me feel like we need to hire security or something to stay in the barn."

Pam laughed. "Now you sound like David. He has been on the phone with the security company for the past hour demanding to know why they cannot install an alarm on the entire property. At the very least, he says we will be installing a security gate with cameras at the front, and cameras around the barn."

Emmy shook her head. "Yea, maybe I should get some more dogs. Let them stay at the barn at night, or something."

Pam considered this. "It wouldn't hurt. Actually, I know a guy who breeds and trains security dogs. They could be kept put up during the day while we are doing lessons and stuff, and then let loose to patrol at night. I'll see what I can do."

Emmy hung up, shaking her head. Glancing down at Rainy who watched her with interest, she shrugged. "Well, we might as well get out there and assess the damage while we wait for the cops to bring our horses back, eh girl?"

Both dogs yipped in response. Emmy wasn't sure how she felt about having trained attack dogs on the property, but she realized that even with Jean-Paul locked up, there would always be the threat of horse thieves with so many expensive horses here at their stables. Pulling on her clothes, Emmy headed out just as the sun was peeking over the barn.

Stopping on the porch to just take in the sight of the sunlight through the clouds, Emmy inhaled the cold morning air. She was lucky she had escaped the assault with her life and much more. One of her biggest fears had come to be a reality with the Frenchman the other day, and Emmy realized that although she was still rattled, she had not slunk into her fear again.

As Emmy surveyed the darkening clouds on the horizon, she felt the breeze pick up. Pulling her coat a little tighter around herself, she whistled to her dogs as she headed out to start morning chores and check for anything amiss after the night's activities. Emmy had only just made it to the training barn when she realized things were most certainly not all right. Every gate stood open, and every stall door inside the barn swayed in the breeze that swirled through the barn.

Emmy groaned. Every single horse on the property had been turned loose. That meant stallions, mares and gelding all ran loose together. Even the gate to the back acreage had been left open. Taking a deep breath, Emmy gathered her emotions. She didn't have time to have a breakdown. There was a lot of work to be done today. Pulling on her gloves, Emmy grabbed a handful of halters and set off looking for the loose horses.

Managing to find and catch about half the missing horses had taken most of her morning, and when the police had arrived with the trailers full of her missing horses, Emmy had to take a break from rounding up the strays to put them away and speak with the police. Altogether, it was a trying morning. As if everything on her plate was not enough, Emmy felt the cold wind blowing in with more gusto as the day wore on.

By late afternoon, Emmy had managed to gather all of the horses and tuck them safely into the barns except one. Standing in front of the empty pasture, watching as the jolly ball spun about in the strong southern wind, Emmy felt herself deflate. She studied the tracks in the mud and had a bad feeling. Judging by the evidence, Wind had been on the list of horses to steal. Emmy guessed the horse had not reacted the way the men had expected, and the colt had gotten spooked and fled.

Emmy felt like crying. She had made so much progress with the colt, and if these guys had chased the fear back into him and undid all of her hard work, she was going to lose it. The colt had already been wary of people, and now, he was probably running loose on the back acreage filled with fear. Pulling her hood up just as the first raindrops began falling, Emmy tossed the halter over one shoulder and whistled for her dogs as she headed into the thick mist descending upon the pastures.

Westley pulled up to the barn, cutting the engine to his truck. Hopping out, he glanced around, looking for signs that anyone was there. The place was eerily deserted. Westley didn't like the silence. He also found it odd that some of the horses were muddy and wet. He could see the empty pastures and knew Emmy must have brought the horses up before the storm, but still, something seemed off.

Walking past the open gate to one of the pastures, Westley frowned. It wasn't like Emmy to be so careless. Even when the pastures were empty she had a strict policy of keeping gates closed. Not seeing any signs of people out at any of the barns, Westley headed toward the house. Maybe Emmy had already gone inside to ride out the storm. He just hoped she was willing to see him when he did find her.

With her ankles sinking into the soggy pasture, the wind ripped at her coat and pulled her hair loose of its braid. Squinting up at the increasingly darkening sky, Emmy frowned. She didn't like the look of things out here. The rain was coming down in a nonstop sheet of cold drops. Rainy and Feather looked miserable. Emmy hoped they would find Wind soon. She would not leave her colt out here in this storm, already spooked by those godforsaken men.

The farther she trudged, the more her worry rose. In the distance, lightning lit up the sky in an erratic display. Emmy knew the chances of thunder were pretty good, and she hoped the colt wouldn't spook even more. Her biggest worry was that the colt could be injured or stuck somewhere. Whistling, and calling for the horse, she prayed her tender bond with the colt would be enough to let him seek her out in his insecurity.

An hour into the storm, Emmy was soaked, exhausted, and starting to lose hope. The sky was so dark, she feared she wouldn't even have enough light to find her way back to the house soon. A shrill whinny split the air, and Emmy's head snapped up. Whirling around, she called out to the horse, hoping to catch a glimpse of his dark coat.

The distraught neigh sounded again, and Emmy realized the horse sounded frantic. When Rainy sprinted off toward the trees, Emmy gathered her soggy clothes and ran after her. Inside the trees, they found the colt, thrashing about, pawing and kicking. The rope around his neck was snagged on a fallen tree, rendering the colt trapped. Emmy sighed with relief both to have found the colt, but also to see him relatively unharmed.

The colt's ears flickered at the scent of the woman he knew. He was frightened, Emmy could see that. Walking slowly toward him, she spoke in soothing tones as she made her way toward him. The colt's entire body shook with anxiety. A flash of white light lit up the sky behind the trees, and thunder shook the earth. The colt spun about, rearing and thrashing as he attempted to get loose. Emmy kept her distance but moved slowly forward. Still cooing softly to the horse, she tried to remind him that he trusted her.

The colt watched her, weary but still wanting the comforting voice and touch of the woman he knew. As she made her way slowly closer to the colt, Emmy reached out with her hand, keeping her body neutral and welcoming. The colt flicked his ears and licked his dark lips. When Emmy saw the horse lower his head slightly, relaxing his posture, she closed the gap between them. Slowly bringing the halter over his nose, she ran her hand soothingly over his neck.

To Emmy's relief, the horse moved into her touch, releasing deep breaths as it sought her comforting touch. Once the halter was secured, Emmy pulled the pocketknife from inside her coat and cut the rope. With the pressure off of his neck, the colt relaxed even more. Emmy just hoped he would trust her enough to walk through the lightning and pounding rain.

The walk back toward the barn was long and cold. The colt was spooked, constantly jumping and lunging forward from the lightning and booming thunder. Emmy was miserable. Her clothes were completely soaked through, and what had originally been a soggy pasture was now a flooded pasture. The water reached the top of her ankles, and now even her boots were not dry anymore. The water and wind made the walk seemed to take three times as long.

One light in the darkness for Emmy was the way the colt responded to her. When he began to give into his natural flight instinct, Emmy would place a soothing hand on him, speaking quietly comforting words, and the colt would calm. Around them, the wind was pelting the rain into them with a fierce sting.

A booming thunder roared around them, and bright lightning struck not too far in the distance. The colt let loose a series of whinnies and reared to full height. Emmy held firm onto the lead, careful to stay out of the colt's kicking radius. Feeling the sting of the rain pelt her harder, Emmy groaned. It was hailing. Gathering the colt, she sprinted toward the direction of the house with the wild colt leaping beside her.

When Emmy heard a whinny in the distance, she looked up just as the rider on the red horse came near. Emmy pulled her unruly colt to a halt, looking up wearily at the rider who approached. In the dark stormy sky, Emmy couldn't make out many details beneath the cowboy hat they wore, but judging by their body, she knew it was a man. It was, however, the deep chestnut horse she recognized first.

Fever. Emmy blinked several times. Who would be riding Bloodfever? The answer struck her with intense force. Westley. With her mind reeling, and questions filling it, Emmy looked up as the rider halted a few feet from her. His features were the same as she remembered, except this time they reflected his worry. His dark green eyes looked her and the horse over.

"Emmy, thank god you're all right. I didn't know what the hell to think when I couldn't find you at the house. When I realized Wind was gone, I didn't know what had happened."

Emmy smiled. Inside, her heart soared at the sight of this man. This one man who seemed to touch something within her she had thought broken.

Tilting her head to the side, Emmy asked, "What, did you think I went for a ride on my wild colt in the middle of a storm?"

Westley frowned. "Yes." He watched the shock, and then the humor color her face. He didn't like the bruise that stained her right cheek, but right now his biggest concern was getting her safely back to the house. "And it's not a storm, you reckless woman. There is a hurricane warning on advisory for the next several hours."

Westley watched as Emmy's face registered shock. So she hadn't known.

"Come on, let's get you home." Emmy frowned as Westley dismounted.

When Emmy sent him a questioning look, Westley sighed. "Must I spell it out for you woman? Get on the horse."

Emmy glanced at the snorting red horse. Hopping up onto the horse, Emmy tried not to let Westley see her surprise as he mounted behind her.

"Give me the rope, and you guide Fever. It'll be easier that way. We need to get you home and dried off. You're freezing."

Emmy didn't argue. Guiding the stallion back toward the house, she allowed him to pick up a canter. She immediately regretted that choice as Westley's hard body crashed with hers in the constant rocking rhythm of the horse's strides. Gritting her teeth, she tried to ignore the sensations igniting within her.

When Westley spoke into her ear, Emmy was grateful for the distraction of conversation. "What the hell were you doing out here with that crazy colt?"

Emmy sent him a warning look. "He's not crazy. I wasn't just out for a stroll in the rain you know."

Westley sent her an amused look. Emmy had the feeling he thought her crazy enough to do just that.

"Why did you come today, Westley?"

"You didn't answer my question. I came to check on you because I heard the advisory. I thought you might be all alone, and I wanted to make sure you and the horses were all right."

"Oh. Thank you. I had to come out here to find the colt. He went missing, and after I had rounded up the others, I realized he must have come out here. I didn't want to leave him in a storm. Good thing too. He had been caught on a fallen tree, the rope around his neck might've strangled him the way he was thrashing about."

Westley was about to respond when her words fully registered with him. "What do you mean rounding up the others? Why did he have a rope around his neck?"

Emmy spent the rest of the ride trying to fill him in on the events of the other day without revealing the assault from Jean-Paul. When Westley rattled off questions, she found it difficult to keep from revealing too much. Relief flooded her when they came to the barn at long last. Relief that she would no longer have to endure the torture of his body rubbing against hers, and relief that she could avoid his questions.

As she led her colt toward a stall in the big barn, Emmy felt herself wondering what would happen now. Would Westley leave, seeing that she and the horses were all right? Would he walk out of her life again, possibly for good this time? Then, her mind wondered other things. Had he met anyone? Had he been with someone, perhaps fallen in love? Emmy tried to shake the questions loose. Grabbing a blanket, she entered the colt's stall and began gently drying the colt.

"Emmy, you need to get in the house, and out of those damp clothes. Let me do that. You're going to get hyperthermia."

The colt snorted at Westley and pinned his ears. Emmy laughed. "I think he just answered for me. I won't be long."

Westley regarded her momentarily. Her dark auburn hair was plastered to her head, and some of it was beginning to curl slightly. Westley smiled. He had always wondered what she would look like wet, he just hadn't expected her to be fully clothed if he ever found out. When Emmy lifted a brow in amusement at his lingering stare, Westley shrugged.

"I closed up all the paddock doors and main doors of the stallion barn. I'll start on the far end of this barn and meet you in the middle. We need to keep everything closed up as much as possible. Are all the horses inside?"

When Emmy nodded, Westley moved off to start securing the building. Sighing, he tried to get his thoughts off of the breathtaking woman he never seemed to stop thinking about. She haunted his thoughts when he was away, and she haunted them now, only a few feet off. Westley didn't have a plan for what would happen now. He only knew he wanted to be here, on this ranch with this woman.

Emmy glanced again out at the barns as she toweled Rainy and Feather off. "Are you sure we shouldn't stay out there with them? How bad is this storm really supposed to be? I thought we were too far inland to be affected severely."

Westley shook his head. "Apparently not this time. They predicted a category three hurricane to hit the entire state of North Carolina. From what I heard on the radio, the storm was making its way much farther inland than anyone had anticipated. They sent out flood and storm warnings to all the counties bordering North Carolina within a hundred mile radius. It's looking to be one of the worst storms we've seen."

Emmy shook her head. "Geez. I hope everyone's prepared. Should I be contacting friends to get the horses moved?"

Westley shook his head. "I don't think so. Your farm is in one of the outer counties, so I think we may get some flooding, but nothing of the evacuation level."

The telephone rang. Emmy picked up on the third ring. "Hello?"

Pam's voice blasted across the receiver, causing Emmy to wince. "OH MY GOD EMMY! I thought you were dead or something! Do you have any idea how long I've been calling?"

Emmy heard Pam call out, "David, its ok, I've got her, you don't have to call the police."

"Pam, I'm all right, I told you earlier that all the horses were out. I have been out rounding them all up, and getting everything closed up for the storm."

"Yes, well, if it was going to take you all day and into a hurricane, you should have let us come out to help like I offered."

Emmy closed her eyes. "Pam, everything is fine, I'm fine, all the horses are put up and safe. I am, however, soaked and I need to get off here so I can go change."

The lights above her flickered lightly, and Emmy frowned. "Pam, I might lose power. The lights just flickered."

Pam cried out. "Geez Emmy! This is exactly why you need a cell! I don't know why you wouldn't let David give you a cell on our plan! That's it. If your power's going to be out and I am not going to be able to know what's going on out there, then I'm coming over!"

Emmy shook her head vigorously. "Pam, no, stay where you're at, I don't want you driving out in this storm with the baby and Topher!"

Emmy's eyes widened when Westley, without so much as asking permission, reached out and took the phone out of her hand.

"Pamela, this is Westley. Yes, I am here with Emmy, I came to check on everything with the storm. No, I don't know why she didn't just tell you that in the first place. Yes, I agree. She needs a cell."

The power flickered again. "You know, I think we are going to lose power any minute. I have my cell on me, you know the number. I will stay with her until the storm's over. You're welcome, Pam. Send my regards to David and…"

Above them, the lights popped as the house darkened and the line went dead. Westley smiled at Emmy and shrugged as he replaced the receiver.

"Well, I guess we are in the dark for tonight. It's odd that the phone line went dead. Perhaps the lines went down in the storm. You got any candles?"

Emmy frowned at Westley. She was still annoyed with him for taking the phone from her.

"Look, Westley, I'm really glad you showed up today, but it's really not necessary that you stay all night."

Westley glanced at Emmy. Remembering the bruising he had seen on her face earlier, Westley felt his anger rise.

"Emmy, what happened to your face?"

Caught off guard, Emmy was suddenly reminded of the bruise marring her face.

"It's nothing, Westley. You're not listening to me. I will be fine. There is no need for you to stay. I'm sure you have better things to do than babysit your ex-boss."

Taking a step toward her, Westley reached out to gently trace the bruise on her face. He knew she didn't want to talk about it, and that only made him more suspicious.

"Emmy, there is nothing more important than being here. Are you going to tell me what happened?"

Emmy bit her lip to still the feelings welling up inside of her at his touch. Shaking her head no, she held his gaze.

"Fine. If you will not tell me what happened, then we will not discuss my leaving here anymore. Now, go change out of those wet clothes while I get a fire going."

Emmy trudged up the stairs. She didn't completely know why she had given in so easily to Westley's instruction. Perhaps it was due to the effect of his hand caressing her face, or maybe it was the feeling of standing in disgustingly wet clothes. Whatever the reason, she retreated to her room with haste. Once inside her room, Emmy began the difficult task of peeling the sticky wet clothes off of her. It took her nearly a half an hour. The jeans were the hardest.

Emmy was still struggling with her jeans when Westley's voice floated to her through the door.

"You know Emmy, I could really use those candles about now. I can hardly see a thing, and I don't know where you keep your lighters or matches."

Emmy froze. She had one leg halfway out of her jeans, and the other she was struggling to pull over her ankle. The only other pieces of clothing on her were the black lace bra and panties. Looking at the door, Emmy realized she hadn't even locked it. He wouldn't just walk in, right?

The door opened, and Westley flashed a light at her. She was frozen with one leg hiked up as she struggled with the pants. Westley froze with the light from his phone pointed at her. Their eyes met, and Emmy felt a shiver run down her spine at the intensity in Westley's gaze. Clearing his throat, Westley turned away.

"Uh, sorry, Emmy. I should have knocked, I just thought you'd be changed by now. That was dumb."

Emmy, caught between embarrassment and humor at Westley's obvious plight, hurried to pull the jeans the rest of the way off. Grabbing her robe, she wrapped it around herself.

"It's all right. I am decent now. Come on, I'll help you find the candles."

Westley peeked over his shoulders. Seeing the black robe she had put on, Westley frowned. She didn't have anything thicker than that? The memory of her black lace undergarments were so scorched into his mind that Westley could practically see them through the thin black material. A branch outside whacked into the side of the house, causing them both to jump.

Westley chuckled, secretly thankful for the distraction. Emmy shrugged. Leading the way, she headed toward the kitchen in hopes of finding a lighter and some candles. Outside, they could hear the storm raging, the wind howling. Emmy paused at a window to assess the barns, worried about the horses. As far as she could tell, both barns seemed to be standing tall against the wind.

She could see the rain that still pelted everything, and about an inch of water had built up on the ground outside. Breathing out slowly, she tried to stay calm. In the kitchen, she searched her cabinets and drawers.

"Ah hah. I knew I had some emergency supplies around here somewhere. Greg must've moved them. Here you go, Westley. One lighter, and several candles."

Westley eyed the small bin full of candles. Taking the lighter, he turned away.

"I'm going to get the fire going or we are really going to freeze tonight."

Lighting a candle to leave in the kitchen, Emmy watched Westley's retreating back. She wondered again why he was really here. After the way he had left, she hadn't thought he would ever want to come back. Much of the fault had been her own, she realized that now. Feeling the cold starting to settle in, Emmy shivered as she followed in Westley's footsteps, ready for the warmth of the fire.

With the fire stirring to life in the large fireplace, Westley glanced at Emmy.

"Speaking of the kid, where is Greg?"

"He's with his family, they've been spending the month in Scotland, visiting relatives, and showing Greg his ancestral home."

Westley nodded. "Ah, I see. That's good. The boy will enjoy it there." Westley trailed off for a minute, looking into the fire. Turning, he lifted a brow at Emmy.

"Your cross-country ride with Dorchadas was phenomenal, Emmy. I don't think I have ever been as effected by a ride before."

Emmy lifted her gaze to Westley's in surprise. "Oh, did you see it on the television? I didn't know it was aired."

Westley held eye contact with Emmy. "No. I watched it in the grandstands. Do you think I would actually miss the opportunity to see you ride my horse in the Grand Prix?"

Emmy was dumbfounded. She was pretty sure her jaw was hanging open. "I...I didn't think you would care after the way things were left between us."

Westley looked away. "I did wonder though, as I sat there watching you, why you didn't choose to ride Fever."

Emmy thought about lying. It would be easier than the truth, and it would reveal a lot less of her real feelings. Studying the handsome man before her, Emmy decided she didn't want to lie. She didn't want hide. It was time she stopped living in fear of what might happen, and live in the hope that something would.

"I couldn't ride Fever in that show. As much as I love that stallion, the truth is, he is your horse Westley. I was reminded of that every time I rode him, and I didn't need that distraction at the Grand Prix."

With his back turned toward her, Westley didn't try to hide the play of emotions that crossed his face at her words. He was overcome with happiness to know his horse had affected her so powerfully. It also meant Emmy had more feelings for him than he had thought.

Turning toward Emmy, Westley looked into her face. He was surprised to see an open expression there, instead of the usual guarded ones.

"Westley, I want to apologize for that day, when I told you to leave. I... well, I didn't really mean..."

Westley stepped forward and placed a finger to Emmy's lips, cutting her apology short. Emmy stared into his eyes, surprised.

"You do not need to apologize for anything, Emmy. I am the fool who owes you an explanation. I should never have walked out on you in a moment of fear when you needed me. I should never have gotten so angry about the horse."

Emmy watched as Westley moved away. She had to admit, she was disappointed that he hadn't tried anything with her.

"The truth is, Emmy, I was scared too. I knew what had happened to you, and I knew I was losing control over my feelings toward you. I should have stopped before it got to the point that it was too much for you. I have never had such a hard time controlling myself as I have with you Emmy."

Turning back to her, Westley watched the surprise on her face. "I wanted you so damn badly. I wanted to be the man who showed you that we are not all the despicable pieces of shit that man who raped you was."

Westley took a step toward Emmy. Keeping his gaze locked with hers, he knew he had to say what he felt.

"Emmy, I have wanted you from the very first moment I saw you riding Viewfinder at the Blue Meadows Grand Prix. The way you moved with your horse, it touched something inside me before I ever even saw your face. When I did, it was even more beautiful than I could have imagined."

Again Westley took a step toward Emmy, until they were mere inches apart.

"When I saw you at the airport, and we had dinner in Ireland, my attraction and curiosity toward you only grew. The three years I spent in Ireland, I could hardly get you out of my mind."

Emmy was both excited and scared. Opening her mouth to speak, she said, "Westley..."

Closing the gap between them, Westley again silenced her with a finger to her lips.

"Emmy, I have loved you since the moment I met you. I just didn't realize it at first. I put off my feelings as physical attraction, but they were so much more than that. When I prodded you into hiring me, it was with the intent of winning your heart. I failed, and I realize I may have messed up my one chance with you, but I need you to know how I felt, how I still feel. When I said there was something here, in America I wanted more than Ireland, it was you, Emmy."

Shock washed over Emmy in strong waves. Outside, the wind battered against the house, the rain thumped continuously against the windows, but Emmy wasn't aware of anything but the man in front of her.

Her voice sounded soft, hoarse when she spoke. "Westley, you didn't fail."

Momentarily unsure what she meant, Westley frowned, but it was Emmy's turn.

"Westley, you didn't fail to win my heart. You did win me over. I have never felt for another man the things I feel for you, and although they still terrify me, I realized too late that I wanted you here."

Westley couldn't believe what he was hearing. Leaning forward, he pulled Emmy into his arms, crushing her against him. With their lips pressed together, and every curve of her body so exposed through her thin robe, Westley didn't know if he could truly control himself. Pulling away, he tried to catch his breath.

"Emmy, I have an incredibly hard time controlling myself around you. There is still a lot I need to say to you, many things I want to share with you, so we need to put some space between us so I can get the chance."

Emmy studied Westley. Her heart raced with the thoughts circling inside her head. She knew they had a lot to speak about still, but in her mind, there was a hurdle that was more important than any words. Willing herself to use every ounce of bravado she contained, Emmy did something she never in her life would have thought herself brave enough to do.

Westley watched the play of emotions crossing Emmy's lovely face. He wasn't sure what was going through her mind. Opening his mouth to speak, Westley nearly choked on his words. Emmy began untying her robe. Westley frowned, unsure what she was doing. When the robe slipped completely off of her, revealing her smooth creamy white skin, covered only by the black lace bra and panties, Westley sucked in a deep breath.

"Westley, I want to hear everything you have to share with me, but right now, the thing I want most is to know what it feels like to make love to a man who loves me."

Westley swallowed. Looking into Emmy's sapphire blue eyes.

"Emmy, are you sure? We don't have to do that yet…"

Emmy stepped forward. Reaching behind her, she unsnapped her bra, letting it fall to the ground. She could see from Westley's expression that he was incredibly affected by the sight of her. Taking things a step further, to show both herself and Westley that she was ready, Emmy slipped her panties off.

Seeing Emmy standing before him, completely naked made Westley realize that she truly was everything he had ever desired in a woman, both physically and mentally. He knew what a huge step this was for Emmy.

When Westley finally reacted, it was to pull Emmy's naked body against him, and kiss her deeply. Emmy felt exposed, excited, afraid, all at the same time. Kissing him back with as much gusto as she knew how, Emmy moaned at the feeling of his hands roving over her. Reaching between them, Emmy tried to unfasten the buttons on his shirt, only to accidently rip one off. Emmy frowned.

Westley, seeing her predicament, laughed. Pulling the shirt off for her, he allowed her to take a good long look.

What Emmy saw was a finely chiseled abdomen and chest. With her nerves wearing thin, Emmy stepped again into Westley's embrace. The more they kissed, the more they touched, the more she wanted. When Westley lowered her to the ground, Emmy didn't feel fear. She felt elation, happiness, love. She truly loved this man, and she wanted nothing more than what was about to happen between them.

Westley couldn't believe what was happening. He was still worried he was moving too fast with her, that he was going to scare her, but as he looked into her eyes, his body pressing hers to the floor, he didn't see fear. Still, his hand hesitated as it trailed up her thigh.

Emmy, sensing Westley's hesitation, looked into his emerald eyes. "It's ok, Westley. Nothing about being with you scares me anymore."

Unable to hold himself at bay, Westley touched her, gently, softly, trying to go as slow as his over-powering need would allow him. She was breathtaking, perfect in every way. There was not one thing about this woman that Westley found unattractive or imperfect. Tracing his hands over her ribs, Westley's fingers felt the small jagged scar on her left side, just below her last rib. Beautiful.

Tracing the raised skin of the scar, he wondered what had happened there. Kissing his way down her neck, over the full curves of her luscious breasts, Westley breathed in the scent of her. Perfect. He didn't know how he had ever gotten so lucky as to be blessed with a woman as amazing as Emmy, but he knew one thing without doubt. He was never leaving her again.

Emmy's breath stuttered as Westley's mouth and hands moved over her body. She sucked in a breath when his teeth grazed her soft skin. Running her hands over Westley's chiseled shoulders, Emmy was overcome with a need, a sensation she didn't know or understand. She cried out when Westley's hand grazed her sensitive areas, and then bit her lip. What would he think of her, making so much noise? As if he sensed her turmoil, Westley found his way back to Emmy's lips.

Whispering against her mouth, he said, "Do you have any idea how much I love it when you make those sounds?"

Emmy laughed. "No, I thought maybe you were afraid this was one of those scenes where I change into a werewolf."

Stopping his perusal of her, Westley lifted himself up on his elbows to peer down at her. After looking at her for a long second, he broke into husky laughter.

"No werewolf, love. More like the most amazingly sexy woman I have ever seen."

Emmy blushed from head to toe. Westley's mouth found hers once again, and Emmy's thoughts dissipated. Not even the thrashing of the southern wind could intrude on her thoughts in that moment. Making love to Westley was like nothing she could have ever imagined. With Westley, there was no pain, no abuse, no taking of something he had no right to take.

Emmy had chosen this. She had chosen to give the most sacred part of herself to Westley, and nothing would ever take the place of being able to make that choice. Making love to Westley, feeling him touch her, kiss her, bring her to the edge of ecstasy, Emmy realized the immense difference between choice and force. She had never imagined she could feel these things she felt, that her body could respond to a man the way it was responding to Westley, and she realized that this choice, this act of making love to someone who loved you was beautiful. Wild. Perfect.

-13-

Opening her eyes, Emmy studied the tunnel of light filtering through the curtains. The warm strong arms wrapped around her reminded her of the amazing night she had spent with Westley. A smile came to her lips. She sorted through her thoughts and memories. After he had made love to her, Westley had sat her down and made her listen to everything he had to say. He told her about his brother, Joseph. About how he held the blame for Joseph's death in his soul and over the head of the red horse for so many years.

Emmy had cried at the story of him losing his brother. She had truly felt his pain and understood why the horse had been such a sore subject. She had cried when Westley told her about watching the video of Joseph's death on the request of his dying mother, and how he had realized the real reason for the accident. Westley even told her that it was his mother's request that he come back here, and follow his heart to Emmy.

Emmy, in turn, had told Westley the entire story of her childhood, of what had happened that night, and thereafter. She also told him the truth of what happened more recently to cause the bruise on her face. Westley had nearly stormed out of the house, intent on killing the Bastard before Emmy could tell him about the police and the horse theft. Once he had calmed down, Emmy also told him about Thanksgiving with her family.

Westley had been happy to hear that she was reconciling her past with them and that they were all apologetic for what had happened so long ago. Then, he had made love to her again. Just thinking about the things they had done brought a blush to Emmy's cheeks. Gently removing the arms from around her, Emmy walked to the window. Peering outside, she was grateful to see that it had stopped raining, and the water outside was only a couple of feet high.

The sky was still dark, but the sun peeked through here and there, doing everything in its powers to chase the remainder of the storm away. As she looked, Emmy felt warm arms encircle her waist.

"You don't think you're going to be getting away from me so soon, do you?" Emmy laughed at the husky Irish lilt in Westley's voice. She had found out that the accent seemed stronger both during sex, and when he was half awake.

"It's five in the morning, Westley. If I am late those horses will tear the barn down. They have a very strict schedule, you know."

Giggling as Westley scooped her up into his arms and proceeded to carry her to the bed, Emmy squealed.

"I'm afraid their breakfast is going to be late today. The future Mrs. Galway has much more important things to attend right now."

Emmy tried not to show her intense reaction to Westley's words. Was he serious? Emmy was still struggling, when Westley sat her on the edge of the bed and disappeared into the bathroom. Emmy frowned, wondering what he was doing. Her question was answered when Westley returned, still completely naked, to kneel before her. Emmy swallowed.

Westley looked up into her alarmed face. "I had a much better plan for this you know, one where I am fully dressed, and everything is perfect and romantic. I realize now, this is perfection at its finest. Being here, with you after last night. I don't want to wait for the right moment Emmy when I have the perfect one now."

Emmy watched in a dazed shock as Westley opened the black box he held in one hand. Staring at the ring, Emmy didn't think she had ever seen anything like it before. The ring was shaped like two horses, wrapping around to embrace one another. In the center sat a heart cut diamond surrounded by small emerald and sapphires. Emmy was completely shocked.

"Emmy, I had this ring made for you three years ago in Ireland. I have had it all this time, just waiting for the moment to ask you. Emmy, will you give me your heart? Will you bless my life by being my wife?"

Emmy swallowed. She stared into Westley's eyes, feeling her own mist up. Nodding, she said, "Oh, god yes. Yes, I will be your wife, Westley."

The honking of a horn brought Emmy out of the stall she was cleaning. Seeing Pam and David's truck coming down the drive with a trailer attached, Emmy frowned. Two weeks had passed since the hurricane, and her friend had been oddly quiet. Emmy hadn't told her about what had happened between Westley and her yet, so she knew her friend was going to be upset.

Hopping out of the truck, Pam waved exuberantly. "Hey Emmy, I brought you a little present."

Emmy frowned. When David stepped out of the driver's side, he looked up, frowning, then he smiled.

"Oh, good, Westley's still here. He can help me with all of this."

Now Emmy was worried. What were these two up to? Walking toward the trailer, she paused as Pam appeared holding the leashes to two incredibly large German Shepherds. Pam grinned at Emmy.

Pointing toward the white dog, she said, "Emmy, I'd like you to meet Frost and Shadow. They are your new guard dogs."

Westley walked up behind Emmy. Studying the dogs, he lifted a brow at Emmy. Glancing back at Pam, seeing her for the first time in almost a year, Westley noticed the small bump on her belly.

"Pam, David, good to see you two again. I didn't know you two were trying for another baby."

Pam blushed, and David grinned. "We weren't. Was a surprise to all of us. A great surprise, but a surprise nonetheless."

Pam waved the two men away. "Why don't you guys go put that kennel together while I introduce the dogs to Emmy and teach her their commands?"

Emmy eyed the dogs. Beside her, Rainy looked about as excited as her. Feather, on the other hand, bounded forward excitedly, licking at the two large dogs submissively. Emmy watched as the two sniffed the little collie with nothing more than curiosity.

"I made sure Roger sent me a pair that would be safe around people and animals. These two are trained to patrol the perimeter, and area around your property. They are safe, unless of course you're trespassing after dark."

Eyeing the pair, Emmy still wasn't sure. She wanted to tell Pam it wasn't necessary now that Westley was here, but she realized horses could be stolen no matter if there was a man here or not. So, she shut her mouth and followed Pam to learn the dog's commands.

Pam watched Emmy with suspicion. It had not escaped her notice that Westley was still here after two weeks. It had also not escaped her notice how happy Emmy looked, or the way she would every so often glance toward Westley and smile. Pam smirked. Her friend was so head over heels in love with the man, she practically glowed with it.

Emmy knew Pam was wondering why Westley was still here, and why she hadn't mentioned any reason behind this. Emmy had a secret, one that both terrified her and made her want to cry with happiness. Looking up at Pam, Emmy smiled.

"You guys busy tonight? Greg comes back tonight, and I thought it would be nice to have dinner with all of us, a welcome home surprise."

Pam smiled. "That sounds nice. It will be good to see Greg again. We would be glad to stay. So, what's up with Westley? He working here again?"

Frowning, Emmy shook her head. "No, well, not really…it's complicated. I'll talk to you about it later, ok?"

Pam sent her friend a vexed look. "Really? Are you trying to kill me with the suspense? That's just not right."

Emmy laughed as she led the dogs toward their newly erected kennel. When she passed Westley, it took everything in her not to reach out and touch him. The look Westley sent her told her he felt the same. Heading into the house, Emmy decided to shower before she started cooking the celebratory dinner she had planned.

With everyone gathered around the dinner table, Emmy pulled the ring from her pocket beneath the table and slipped it onto her finger. Feeling for Westley's hand where he sat beside her, she gave it a squeeze. Standing up, Emmy cleared her throat. When everyone had quieted down and looked up at her, she spoke.

"First off, I'd like to welcome Greg home. This place has been far too quiet without you. Besides, I have missed the incredible meals of our future chef."

Everyone around the table laughed. "Secondly, I want to share some news with you all. Everyone here tonight I consider family. You have all been there through the hardest times of my life, and you've never let me down. That's why I know the news I'm about to share will make each of you incredibly happy."

Emmy paused to allow her words to sink in. She certainly had everyone's attention. Glancing down at Westley, she lifted her brows. Taking the hint, he pushed his chair back to stand beside her.

"Westley has asked me to marry him, and I've accepted."

The room erupted with shouts and cheers, and Emmy couldn't hide the smile that came to her face. Turning to face Westley fully, Emmy held up her hand for silence.

When all was quiet, she looked into Westley's eyes, and said, "And, I am pregnant."

∞∞∞∞

ABOUT THE AUTHOR

Brandy L Cunningham lives in California with her husband and two children. She is an animal lover and has spent her life working with horses. She has an Associate Degree in Animal Science and has four published novels. To learn more, visit her at Facebook.com/blc.author